Down Sterling Road

NELLIE McCLUNG

Down Sterling Road

a novel by Adrian Michael Kelly

Coach House Books, 2005

first edition

Published with the assistance of the Canada Council for the Arts and the Ontario Arts Council. We also acknowledge the Government of Ontario through the Ontario Book Publishing Tax Credit Program and the Government of Canada through the Book Publishing Industry Development Program.

LIBRARY AND ARCHIVES CANADA CATALOGUING IN PUBLICATION

Kelly, Adrian Michael, 1967-
    Down Sterling Road / Adrian Michael Kelly. – 1st ed.

ISBN 1-55245-157-7

    I. Title.

PS8621.E44D69 2005   C813'.6   C2005-905595-2

In memory
of
Patrick Joseph Kelly,
my Dad,
March 16, 1938–April 30, 2003

The life of everybody is a road to himself. ... No man has ever yet attained to self-realization, yet he strives after it, one ploddingly, another with less effort, as best he can. Each one carries the remains of his birth, slime and eggshells, with him to the end.

— Herman Hesse, *Demian*

There is no more to do
But to turn and go away,
Turn and finally go
From one who was much to me,
Nothing to anyone else.
Often it must be so
And always words be false.
Child, do you blame what is?
Child, do you blame what was?

— Sydney Tremayne, 'A Burial'

ONE

Already awake, and curled like a busted C, Jacob has just taken his hands from his ears when Dad thumps the bedroom door and says Up.

Two secs, Dad.

Had an extra half-hour already. Let's *go*.

Jacob hides his eyes, turns the lamp on. Rolls over. Almost a whole year now since Cornelius Waldengarden got Dad into running. Johnny Johnny, let me tell you, big boy, it's absolutely great exercise.

To watch them slog it round the old horse track up beside the arena almost hurt at first. Thick spit stuck to Dad's huff-puffing lips. His slow heavy strides, like the ground wouldn't let him lift his feet. Neily slowing down for him, jogging backwards. C'mon, Johnny McKnight, move those bones. Shut yer gob, Waldengarden. Jockeys on the trot flicking whip sticks and clucking their tongues and having a laugh, look at these wackos, who in hell runs round a dirt track at seven in the morning? Every day. Even Sundays. With Neily, without Neily. Like something inside Dad sprouted. Down to Belleville for new shoes, track suits. Running logs, electrolytes. It's got hold of me, son. Interval training, speed work. Johnny, Johnny, you're looking great, boy. And by spring it's Neily still driving down to the horse track for laps and Dad driving down the Sterling Road to spray-paint mile markers on the telephone poles and the pavement – three, then five, then six miles out. And back.

And Jacob with him since summer. Every day. Can't go as far, Dad, hurts my knees. Boy, I've told you, this sport is about your mind, and Dad tap, taps his temple. Good name for a body part, *temple*, it's what running is for Dad now.

Whump on the door. *Hey, I said up.*

Jacob sits up and says sorry twice. Rubs his eyes. Breathes out *phooh*. It's Saturday. Hill day.

He shivers out of his PJS, into his sweats. Will need his nylon shell as well. Ice on the bedroom window.

In the kitchenette, Dad's waiting at the table, shell on and all. 'Bout bloody time, he says.

Sorry, says Jacob.

And Dad points his chin at the kitchen counter. Get stretched.

Jacob nods, lifts his left heel to the countertop. Leans, and counts in whispers, *one* one thousand, *two* one thousand, as Dad gets the electrolytes mixed. They taste like soap and go half-slush in the cold, make Jacob gag. He swallows, hard.

What's the matter, boy?

Just tired.

Look half-dead.

Didn't sleep too good.

You'll be wide awake by the time we hit they hills.

Jacob nods.

Right, that's us. Get your shell on and we're out the door.

Jacob tugs and zips and ties drawstrings. Steps into his Nikes. Could gag right now. Beginning – it's almost as bad as hills. Butterflies, bad, till you get going. Then it's okay. Can even be good, but mostly when Dad's not there and Jacob can go his own pace, have a look round, when the sun comes up, at all the colours only mornings have.

Double knots, kid, we'll have no more stopping to tie bloody laces.

Jacob nods, ties tight.

And that's them down the stairs, out the lobby, into the dark and hush. Still pitch-black almost. Cold. Jacob shivers – Buck up, boy, it's no that bad – and jumps on the spot to get a peek round Dad and across the road into Chuck Linton's yard. Hears Teddy's chain *clink* and *clank* against the doghouse, but can't see him behind Chuck's big shitty flatbed truck. Jacob puckers, makes a kissy sound. And Teddy barks like it's at the moon.

Wake up the whole town, why don't you?

Sorry.

Hope you're staying away from that mutt.

Yeah.

Half-mad, that thing.

Just lonely.

See if I care. He'll go for you like he went for bampot Linton. Stay away, y'hear me?

Jacob nods and kneels and pretends to pull the tongues of his shoes so Dad can't read his face. He's been sneaking over to Linton's lot with bologna or a leftover banger since Grade Seven started. Talks nice, tells Teddy it wasn't his fault. It was an accident.

Right then?

Jacob nods.

Dad – *beep* – hits the stopwatch. We're offskee.

And Jacob checks his shoulder.

Teddy, quiet now, watches them going like it's for good.

Keep up, kid.

Jacob, *phooh*, lengthens his stride. Dad goes out hard the first couple of blocks. Jump-starts the system, he says, lets it know what's what.

They turn off Victoria, onto Brock, then settle into a medium-slow pace. Saving it for the hills. Jacob breathes into his belly and – he could run the route blindfolded – closes his eyes. Opens them *blink* just as they pass Immaculate Conception – looks nice in the dark and the hush, without all the buses and kids – and then *blink* the chocolate factory. Night-shift folks filing out. Lunch boxes and laughing, cigarettes like fireflies. A few people wave and say Morning or Get there faster if you drove, Johnny, and Dad laughs and waves but looks down and says Keep fucken smokin and I'll be drivin you to hospital, smartarse.

Jacob picks it up a bit to make like he's not interested, but has a quick look back. Sun-up the factory looks dumpy for being so famous, but in the dark it looks, if you want it to, like a painting, an old painting, of a dark castle. The kind of painting you swear is breathing, and invites you in.

Okay, kid, let's get goan.

Dad pulls back alongside as they turn onto Sterling Road, into blowing snow, and their shells lash and snap like flags.

Get that head up.

Hurts the eyes, Dad.

Made of sugar?

No.

Then get your head up.

Jacob squints and blinks, blinks and squints.

And Dad says Let me by then. Moves in front. Usually breaks the wind on bad days.

On they go past the beer store and the Hydra restaurant and the old sign Welcome to Glanisberg, Apple Core of Ontario, Population 400, except it should be 4000 but the last zero fell off and no one gives a crap. Most of the orchards are gone, and Glanisberg is way more famous for the factory anyway. You can even buy Cook's chocolate in Australia because of the new boss – hardly anybody ever sees him, just his flash Jag with the tinted windows, and he's not even in the Cook family. He's American. And everybody says he's changing the way business gets done around here. Started with his own office. Jacob saw pictures in the *Herald* – swanko – and he's not sure why exactly but he wants *in* there, in the boss's office.

But the Murph won't let them in.

The mailbox – Jacob can read it from here – used to say THE MURPHYS back when. When his wife was alive. And when his kid was still there. Then he put duct tape over the S and the Y. Some people say it was Children's Aid had to come. Dad says people should mind their garbage mouths, stop talking daft crap all the time. Still crosses the road, though, whenever they run by and says – here it comes – Watch for dogs.

Dad, we've never seen them even once.

Take half your leg off, says Dad, snapping his head like a dog's got hold of a groundhog. And if they come for you when I'm no here, don't –

I know. Don't run.

Stand your ground, smartarse. Or they'll get you *here* – Dad dips down and pinches Jacob's Achilles tendon, makes torn skin and tissue sound. Right the fuck out they'll take it, and that's you hobbled. Never heals.

Jacob nods and swallows and blinks away the feeling of teeth on his tendon. Thinks of Teddy. Dad was dead wrong about him. Maybe he's dead wrong about the Murph's dogs, too. Might not be friendly with everybody, but probably pals for the Murph, up there alone in a falling-down farmhouse. Dean Spielman, mean Dean, speedy Dean, says the guy's just a pervert. Spielman should know. Except for the back of hockey cards, all he reads is *Hustler* magazines his dad leaves lying around the greenhouses. *Pornography* is Greek and means *writing about prostitutes.*

Kid.

Eh?

Away with the fairies.

Just thinkin.

About what?

Nothing.

You sure?

I'm sure.

So get a move on. And get this in you. Dad passes him the electrolytes.

It's cold, Dad, I'm fine.

You're still losing fluids. Drink.

Jacob drinks. Swallows a gag.

You right then? says Dad.

Jacob nods. Passes the electrolytes back.

Okay, kid, pick it up a bit.

They make the turn into Harris Provincial Park, jump the gate chain and turn left.

Here come the hills.

Jacob closes his eyes, puts a soft *please* in his out breath.

Lean into her, boy.

Trying, Dad.

Faster.

And then they come, like moths in his skull, smacking the backs of his eyes.

Dull dead eyes but open like saints' in pictures.

Attack it, son.

Martyred and mortified and looking –

Come on, move.

– up at God like he'll never let the pain end.

Get that head up.

And bits of skin and tissue, stuck to the sawtoothed pedal spinning this way, that way, this way –

Breathe, fucksakes.

Jacob spits and gulps air and tries to settle his breath, settle his breath, but stabbing the bits keep stabbing his eyes.

Bone bits, and Dad's bloody hands.

Stay with me, son.

One and *two* and squelching like a sopping squeezed sponge.

Are you breathing, boy?

And Mrs. Simpson crying black smears *O John he came out of nowhere I swear.*

They crest, and drop their arms for the downhill.

Let it go, kid.

Johnny, let it go, Johnny, let him –

Jim, you stop and I'll fucken kell you, I swear.

I can't, Dad.

Come on, boy.

Dad, I can't.

Yes, you can, now come on.

I'm gonna be sick.

Be sick if you like. You'll take the next hill.

Slow, Dad, please, I'm – Jacob gags – sick. And he stops, hands on knees, breath in heaves.

Boy, I cannot believe you.

I'm sorry, Dad, says Jacob, standing straight and getting – *bumpf* – a water bottle right in the chest.

Dad's face. Boy, he says, fucksakes. I've no idea. I mean, what gets into you?

Jacob looks down, rubs his chest.

Nothing, is it? says Dad. Have you nothing in you? 'I'm sick.' Full of piss and vinegar yesterday.

Just the hills, Dad.

Eh? Speak up. I said speak up.

Jacob can't talk. Just picks up the water bottle. Hands it back.

Guess you'll be walkin home then.

I'll give them a go tomorrow, Dad, I swear.

Tomorrow. Never fucking mind, tomorrow. It's what you do today. How d'you expect to win anything without increasing your speed, your –

Endurance.

But Dad – *Ach* – just waves him off, and starts running back.

Jacob watches him until he crests the hill. Then runs after him, hard.

Rest of the morning Dad goes to his room. Says he needs to study. Jacob goes to his room, too. Slides a stack of comics out from under the bed. *Iron Man. The Flash.* And *Green Lantern.* Can't read that one. Can't read any of them. Even in bed under the covers bits keep coming. June 21. The Bairns' Big Day. Icing. And you sing. Everyone okay.

> *Happy birthday to you,*
> *Happy birthday, you two,*
> *Happy birthday, dear*
> *JACOB*
> *A*
> *I*
> *L*
> *A*
> *N*
> *Happy birthday, you two.*

Phooh!

Eighteen candles *poof,* nine either end. But Jacob didn't blow. Jacob didn't wish. Said no to cake and – *You spoiled little bugger* – just stared at his dish. Because his bike was different. Was supposed to be the same. Every year before – toys or clothes or trikes and bikes – they always got the same. Mum said *Stop your bloody grumbling*. But the bikes changed the game. Their favourite secret game. Criss-cross *Go* down the subdivision hill.

You're me!

I'm you!

Faster!

You, too!

Skid like a C the other way round, skid like a J but upside down. Then smack the stop sign, and do it one more time. A thousand times they did it, almost every single day. Cailan never traded. And cars hardly came.

Except the day after Halloween. Pumpkins still on porches. Windows needing cleaned.

Please, Cailan, trade?

Just to spook him was all. He never knew. Jacob's back tire. He can still see it. Worn almost through. Just one time. To spook him. If the tire even blew.

We should go to the hospital, Jacob, Dad'll brain us if we're late.

Just one more time, Cailan, cross my heart it's true.

Jacob knocks his fists together, whispers Stop it, stop it, please. But he hears the *bang* like yesterday. Bites his hand. Thumps his knee. *Bang* like a backfire, *bang* like a gun. Here comes the car. And that sound – Jacob slaps his ears – of skin, and metal. Scraping along road.

The rest is bits. Pieces. And, in between, big white blanks.

Jacob. *Jacob.*

Rubs his eyes. Yeah, Dad?

Lunchtime.

Dad's doled out the Chunky Soup and has his big ambulance book on the table. He's studying for his EMCA exam: Emergency Medical Care Assistant. Let's go, kid, quiz me.

'Kay.

Jacob stands the book one half either side of his bowl, and between mouthfuls of Beef Veg – Dad put Lea & Perrins in – asks him questions about procedure. Subdural hematomas. Puncture wounds. Dad gets them all bang on but one: during CPR, intubation is recommended when there is excessive blood in the lungs.

Spoons, the sugar bowl and Jacob jump when Dad *bang* hammers the table and says I fuckingwell *knew* that.

It's okay, Dad, you got almost perfect.

But Dad doesn't hear, really, just says like a secret Should have fuckingwell known, and goes to his room. He won't come out for a long while.

Jacob sits on his hands. Stares at the gleam on the edge of the table, at the sugar that splashed out the bowl.

The phone's on its fourth, fifth ring and through the door Dad yells *Get* that.

'Lo?

Asalamalakim ...

Jacob's shoulders drop. It's Graham Hollingsworth. Except everyone calls him Cracker mostly because of his first name because even when he makes like black dudes from the TV – What's *hatnin*, you *jive*-ass turkey? – he talks slow as molasses.

Not much hatnin, Cracks. What you doing?

Factory ... You wanna come?

Who's all going?

Just us ... guys.

Spielman?

Yeah.

Jacob looks at Dad's closed door. Should maybe stay in, he says.

How come?

Read.

It's Christmas break ... sucka.

He won't let us in anyway.

Never know. You comin or not?

... Guess so.

See you there.

'Kay.

Fingers in his pockets, out his pockets, Jacob steps this way that way in front of Dad's door. Listens. No snoring.

Dad. Dad?

Eh?

Going outside.

Careful.

Will.

Jacob gets his togs on. Rummages through the junk drawer in the kitchen. Finds a safety pin for the busted zipper on his coat. Takes the stairs quiet. Jogs, hands in pockets, all the way to the factory, cold coming through the tear in his armpit. Out back the factory Dean Spielman says Nice coat, for the umpteenth time. Jacob just blows on his hands, does a dude shake with the Cracks. Bobby Hollingsworth, Graham's little brother, takes a haul on his puffer and says Colder than a witch's tit out here.

Shouldn't feel anything under all that fat, says Spielman, and Bobby flips the bird at his back when the Deaner turns and knocks on the black back door. Knocks again. Loud.

He always answers, but just opens the door a crack. You can see one eye. Part of his big bald head with the splotch on it. The scar on his lip. Teeth. *You* again?

Bobby always looks like he's going to shit his pants but it's him who says Us again.

Told you a hundred times, porker, don't give tours anymore.

Let a bunch of other guys in last week, says Spielman.

Who.

Garth Hutchinson. Lyle Bunyan.

Liars.

We saw it.

Saw *what*.

The chocolate, says Jacob. You gave it them.

And what are you gonna give me, eh, little runner boy?

Jacob looks down. But Spielman says Give ya two bucks.

The Murph laughs. Two *dollars. Rich* boy. Get outta here. Freeloaders –

Are not, says Bobby, but his voice and face are shaky –

Little cocksuckers, says the Murph, *out* of here! And everybody jumps.

Boom. Door closed.

Holy motha, says Cracker, bending with his hand on his heart. Thought he was gonna grab one of us.

I'd hoof him in the balls, says Spielman. Fucken pervert. Let's go.

It's not true, says Jacob.

Is so. Lyle Bunyan brought him a *Penthouse.* That's how he got in.

Lyle Bunyan talks daft crap. And anyway your dad reads *Penthouse.*

Ours, too, says Bobby, nodding and nodding and the ball on his toque bobbling and bobbling. Then he takes another haul on his puffer.

And Cracker hits him in the shoulder. Mum said just one pump, dumbo.

Have to *breathe,* asswipe. That *hurt.*

This hurt? says Dean, and he nails Bobby's other shoulder. Jacob pictures nailing Spielman – right *smack* on the jaw, like Dad shows – except Spielman's mum always gives Dad good deals on flowers. Plus Jacob's hands, they've gone half-numb.

Let's just go tobogganin, says Cracker, and Bobby says Yeah! like no one ever hit him.

McKnight can't go tobogganin, says Spielman, he doesn't have one.

Can borrow mine, says Cracker.

It's okay, says Jacob. I should go home. My dad –

Needs you to cook dinner? says Spielman.

Shut up, Dean.

Make me. Dean stops walking. *Make* me.

Cracker stops.

Bobby stops.

But, Jacob – *Ach* – waves them off.

Yeah, Dean yells, run.

Jacob just keeps going.

I could catch you from here if I wanted!

Jacob keeps going.

Faster.

And doesn't stop till he's at the top of the stairs, his hands over his stinging ears. Stuffing falling out his armpit. Hard to turn the key in the lock. Hard to hold the key. Has to use two hands.

Just when Jacob comes in, Dad comes out of the bathroom. Looks like he woke up from a thousand years, but eyes Jacob up and down, says Look at the sight of you, boy.

Heat prickles Jacob's face. Fingers, tingling. I'm okay, Dad.

Okay nothing. It's bitterly cold out there. That's you Monday, new togs.

Sundays are distance. Long, slow distance. Past the park. Past Potts' farm. Almost to the big limestone house that belonged to the dead lady doctor who left all the books to the Glanisberg library. Jacob's been meaning to get down there. And will, tomorrow. The library's right next to the Sally Ann. Meantime, get the head up, boy. Focus. Replenish your fluids. Maintain your form.

Dad holds the jeans to Jacob's waist, lets the legs flop flop down. Jesus Christ, boy, will you *stop*?

What?

Groan, you're groan like a weed.

One of the little old ladies who minds the thrift shop looks up from her hemming. Hard to believe the size of him, John.

Eats me out of house and home, love, house and home.

Can't keep him in clothes that fit, I'm sure.

Dad folds the Levi's, grabs GWGS. No point in buying him new, dear. Kid grows so quick the clothes'd be down here before he wore them thrice.

No harm in second-hand, John, isn't that right, Jeanie?

The other old lady just nods and folds a T-shirt and Dad says Right you are, love. Eyes the hem, speaks lower. These'd be about right, no, son?

Jacob looks along his leg and says Guess so.

Go and try them on then, while I have a look round.

'Kay.

On his way to the changing area, Jacob keeps an eye on Dad, wonders if he still looks, too. Just last spring Jacob thought he saw the green pullover. Hanging there. Nothing where feet and hands and a face should be. Just holes. Could have kept all those clothes. All of them. Worn them. But *boom* Dad pounded the patio table. *Bugger* it, it's down the Sally Ann with the lot, the *lot*. And he broke down the other bed and yanked the drawers right out and stuffed garbage bags. That one's mine, Dad. How would I bloody know, there's two the same of everything. The name tags, Dad, Mum wrote C on his. What'd she write on yours? Nothing.

Jacob blinks hard, draws the big bone-white curtain, steps out of his trainers. Sock feet cold against the concrete floor, he unzips and shivers and tosses his trousers over the rickety stool. Between the gap in the curtains he sees Dad looking through the winter coats, this one no, that one no, this one maybe, then he stops, holds up the sleeve of a Toronto Argos jacket, takes a quick look at the tag. Makes like he's not had a fright when the old lady with the needle and thread says Goose down, John.

Eh, too small for that galoot of mine. Dad points toward the curtains and Jacob ducks away. Pulls on the jeans. Looks down his legs. Sees his ankles. At school Dean Spielman'll point and laugh and ask Jacob when the flood is coming.

Son?

Yeah, Dad?

How's it goan in there?

They fit okay.

Let's have a look at you.

Jacob gets the sticky zipper up, steps out.

Dad has a look. Those'll do you till spring.

Jacob just nods.

Right, says Dad, come on over here a minute.

Jacob follows him to the coat rack.

What do you think of these then?

One I have still fits.

Give your head a shake, boy, that thing's a goner. I was thinking this'd do you.

Dad picks the exact coat Jacob knows he will but hopes he won't. A green hunting jacket, reversible, with a wide tail that covers your bum. Stain like oil down the left side. The hunting side is bright orange like Dad's ambulance parka. Dad hides his mouth with his hand. 'Sonly five dollars, he whispers. Get it on you and we'll have a look.

The sleeve ends brush Jacob's fingernails but Dad says At the rate you're groan, it'll be bang on come next winter. Then he wrings Jacob's arm just above the elbow and in the old ladies' direction says Real goose down in this one as well. Warm as it gets, eh love?

Warm as it gets, John. Do you like it, dear?

Jacob says It's super, ma'am, but just wants to put his old clothes back on and get out the frigging door. Whenever he and Dad need new gear it's top of the line. Brooks. Adidas. Got tae buy what lasts, kid. Protect yourself from weather, and injury. But for normal clothes they always come back to this sad cold cellar that smells like holes and old people.

Best be on our way, kid, I'm workin afternoons.

Jacob changes, listens to Dad carrying on with the old ladies. Slow as molasses in January, that boy is. Not many in town can keep up with you, John. Aye, that's me, the Flying Scotsman. When the old ladies laugh it sounds like wheezy seagulls. Yepsir, real goose down. And who notices a little stain, John?

Then it's quiet. And Jacob can feel their eyes on him – *Poor boy, isn't that a pity* – as he and Dad head for the stairs.

Outside, Dad says Hello there to the Sally Ann man ringing his little bell by the money ball. Someone put in a whole two-dollar bill. Dad drops a quarter in and says All the best to you.

The Sally Ann man tugs the peak of his cap and says God bless.

Jacob jogs ahead. Jumps up the steps to the public library. Presses his face against the window. The dead lady doctor left the library a huge big dictionary. Twelve volumes. Plus art books with

Dali and Picasso. Jacob wants a look before Mrs. Bailey the librarian covers up the pictures like pornography. But she won't let Jacob or anyone see anything until all the books have been cleaned and catalogued and shelved.

Jacob raps on the glass.

Mrs. Bailey looks *shoo* over her specs and her mouth makes the words *my window*.

Jacob tugs his sleeve over his palm and gives the glass a rub. Jumps down all the stairs *smack*.

Here's Dad, shaking his head. Break your ankle, he says.

It's not high.

Weak bones.

Drink that calcium stuff every day.

I mean in your ankle. Anyone's. Fragile.

They shouldn't be.

Tell me about it.

Dad?

What.

Do you know what her real name was?

Who?

The dead lady doctor out the Sterling Road.

Henderson.

What Henderson?

Eh?

Her first name.

What do you care?

Just asking.

Trudy.

That's Mum's name.

No need to tell me that.

They have the same name?

Think your mother owns it?

No ... She left all these books to the library.

Who did?

The doctor. Art books and everything and a dictionary that has every single word in it.

Go friggin blind, you will.

I can see perfect.

Bloodywell hope so. Think I can afford glasses?

No, says Jacob, kicking a small stone down the sidewalk.

Dad digs the car keys from his pocket, sniffs the air like someone did a fart and says Jesus Murphy, factory smells something awful today. Didn't lock your side, I see.

Sorry.

You're always sorry. Get in.

When they get back to Hillcrest Heights there's poor Teddy across the road, out in the wet snow, no food in his bowl and howling. Inside, Dad takes the radio to the bathroom so he can listen to repeats of *The Goon Show* when he's having a shower. But the reception's bad so he just whistles like the Black Watch Pipes and Drums. Jacob shuts his bedroom door and tries to read *X-Men* but can't concentrate. Dumps the jar out on his bed, counts his allowances. Figures how much he'll have left over after he buys Luciano Pavarotti for Dad. Maybe he can get Teddy a bone from Rick the butcher at $harpe's $uper $ave. A huge big femur. Sneak it over. Teddy can gnaw at it all he likes. Bury it. Dig it up again in springtime.

Jacob slides the jar back under the bed. Gets some paper and the pencil stub from his nightstand. Draws bones. Human bones. An elbow joint. An ankle. A femur. Then Dad pops his head in. That's me away.

'Kay.

What are you drawing there?

Bone.

Can see that. What's it called?

Femur. Largest in the body.

Correct.

A lot of weight-bearing responsibility.

Aye, so don't sit on your arse all night.

Won't.

Get some food in that belly of yours.

Will.

Lovely piece of fish in the fridge. Perch.

'Kay.

Some spuds and peas with it, not a bad wee nosh.

Sounds good, Dad.

Time you had a haircut, too. Look like a mop.

Not that skinny.

Skin and bloody bone, boy.

Jacob breaks the point of his pencil but makes it look like an accident.

Dad stares at it, the pencil, for a sec, two, then he's out the door and away down the stairs.

Jacob eyes the hole at the end of his pencil. Listens till he can't hear the Gran Torino anymore. Crawls under the covers. Hopes the rest of December comes and goes like a heartbeat.

But the days don't come and go like heartbeats, they slow down like the middle of a long run when you feel the wall coming on and just want to stop. Except, like Dad says, you're so far down the road what the hell else are you gonna do except keep plodding on – like the second hand of the clock on Christmas Eve, it looks like it's ready to pack it in when Dad finally calls at six and says Sorry, son, I'll be a wee while yet.

How come?

Patient transfer.

Peterborough?

No. Serious. Kingston General.

You're on days tomorrow, Dad. Supposed to be you gets to come home.

On-call guy's got flu, Dad says, then he puts, Jacob can tell, his hand over the phone before he tells Jim Digby I can't believe this kid. Jim laughs then Dad comes back on and says See you, don't wait up.

'Kay.

After he hangs up, Jacob wraps the Luciano Pavarotti tape, leans it against the tree stand. Plugs in the lights. The old tree still looks pretty in the dark.

Gets half his spaghetti down. Tosses the rest. Dishes done. Teeth brushed like they show you in school, but his gum still bleeds. Cavity's the size of his fingertip now. He dabs Dad's Orajel on it. Gets into his PJs, bed. Leans over a pile of *X-Men*. Reads and listens for the front door and the footfalls, but his eyes get heavy, sore. Light off.

Flat on his back, Jacob makes prayer hands on his forehead. Closes his eyes. Breathes *phooh* and says I know we don't go to church anymore or anything and I don't want to be selfish so even if Dad didn't get me Prismacolor pencils that's okay, please just let us have a good Christmas. It's the third one now.

Then he rolls, and curls, and breathes way down into his belly.

Back at the old house by the river Dad used to climb on the roof and stomp around Ho ho ho, not *asleep* yet? and for a second, two, Jacob thinks he hears it. But it's not. It's just Dad with the lights left off, bumping into furniture and swearing on his way to the stereo. In the hush and dark Jacob hears everything – the *soosh* of the record being slid from its sleeve, the needle's hiss and the speakers' crackle heartbeats before the story begins. *One Christmas was so much like another* ... booms the big warm voice, and Dad cranks the sound down, but Jacob knows the words ... *in those years around the sea-town corner now and out of all sound except the distant speaking of the voices I sometimes hear a moment before sleep* ...

Even when Jacob and his brother couldn't understand the words, when they just liked the sound of the big warm voice, Dad always played Dylan Thomas on Christmas Eve – *Listen, boys* – and drank hot toddies and honey with Mum. Now he listens alone, to all of it, twice. Lets the record keep playing at the end – *t-chikt, t-chikt* – goes to the fridge and gets more ice. Jacob, heart hammering, can picture everything – the tree, blinking on, blinking off, and Dad on the sofa, drink about to spill, staring at the blank TV. Please let him go to bed, he's working tomorrow and he needs a good sleep.

The clock flips *click* from 4:59 to 5:00 and Jacob's eyes blink open again. He stays still, listens to the dark and the hush. Then hears Dad's apnea. Lies there some more. Dad snorts, makes daft sounds. Goes quiet again. At quarter to six Jacob gets out of bed, picks up the tin wastebin in the corner of his room. Waits for a snort then drops the bin *clang*. But Dad just snuffles and groans.

Wake up, Dad. Wake *up*.

At six Jacob says to himself Just a quick look-see. Ever so slowly opens his bedroom door. The dark apartment like held breath, streetlight glow through the windows. Cold linoleum against the balls of his feet as he closes his eyes except for a slit and sneaks to the living room.

And opens his eyes.

Two presents. Dad's, and another one. About the size of a sketchbook. Jacob sneaks over to give it a shake, but jumps when Dad's alarm clock buzzes. Spins and takes big quiet steps back to his room.

Dad hits the button and makes big wake-up noises like he's been dragged by the heels into the world and isn't too sure he wants to be here because it's all bangers and mash and bodies on stretchers.

Jacob, breath held, waits just inside his bedroom door.

Waahhh, y'up, son?

Jacob fakes a yawn. Pardon, Dad?

Dad laughs. I heard you.

Me?

Who else could it have been, I wonder.

Don't know, Dad.

It's quiet, then Dad says What day is it today, son?

It's Christmas, Dad.

Christmas? Well, Jesus Joseph and Mary it is. Guess I'll sleep in then.

Can't, Dad, you're on days.

Is that right, now? Well, in that case.

The wait. Then Jacob mouths the words when Dad sings O how happy I would be, if I hadda cuppa tea!

First tea. Then prezzies. The way it always was. Jacob uses the special yellow mug with the red lion rampant on it.

Here's Dad tying his robe, hair like a messy nest. Well, my favourite mug and all. Thanks, son.

Welcome.

Careful not to spill, Dad takes a stool from the kitchenette, plunks it down by the tree. Jacob sits on the floor. One of the gold balls has fallen off a bottom branch.

Eh, hang on a minute, son. Wee repair job here.

Dad loops the string round some bristles, bends the branch's wire a bit. There we are, he says, right as rain. Now then, what have we here, ho ho.

Jacob points, says That one's for you.

Dad picks up the little present, reads the sticker. To: Dad From: your son Jacob. Guess I'm no on Santa's list again this year.

Jacob shrugs, tries to smile. His face heats when Dad starts popping Scotch tape.

Grand wrapping, son.

Did it myself.

Dad tears the paper. Hey hey, Luciano Pavarotti!

I was gonna get you pipes and drums. Black Watch. But it's hard to find ones you don't have.

No, son, this is great. Your dad loves old Looch.

Jacob looks at the other present.

Dad reaches for it, says Well then, here you are.

Thanks, says Jacob. He picks it up. To Jacob, Merry Xmas, love Dad.

Dad nods, blows on his tea. Slurps, his eyebrows like drawn bows, then swallows and tries not to smile. But his front tooth shows.

Jacob looks away, pops tape.

I'm no expert wrapper like you, Dad says.

It's really good, Dad, says Jacob, thinking that the sketchbook's no cheapy. It feels thick, heavy.

Son, I'll no be saving the paper.

Sorry. Jacob tears. And stops, when, in the book's bottom corner, he sees a skeleton hand but coloured in pink and gold.

Dad bobs his eyebrows.

Jacob tears more paper, sees another hand. A live hand, with a hairy thumb, holding a skinny marker and colouring the drawing of the bones.

Holy, Dad, what *is* this?

Look and see.

Jacob pulls on the book's bottom edge and the flaps of paper fall away.

The Anatomy Coloring Book?

Now, what do ya think o' that, kid!

Jacob swallows.

Couldnae believe that when I saw it. It's perfect for you, son. *Slurp, gulp.* Something missing, is there?

No. It's great, Dad. Thanks.

Dad sets his tea down, looks out the window. His Adam's apple bobs. I know it's Christmas and all, he says, staring between the curtains. Then he looks back at Jacob – hard – and says But let me say this anyway. Son, it's not your drawing I mind. You know I wasn't too bad with a brush meself once.

Jacob hunches, stares at Dad's shins.

Son, look at me. You like your drawing, that's great. Really, it is. But all they comic book, wam-bam pictures and whatnot.

Fantasy art, Dad.

Whatever they call it, you're gettin too old for all o' that stuff. Eleven?

Aye, and goan on twice that sometimes.

Jacob looks away, swallows.

Son, listen to your old dad. Look at me. You've got a talent, there's no one gonna deny that. Neily Waldengarden's seen it, too, knows like I do you've got some grey matter in that noggin. Dad leans forward and raps Jacob's head like a door. *Use* it, son, is what I'm saying.

Jacob's left nostril twitches.

Son, I've told you, you don't wanna end up like your old dad, driving bloody ambulance. You could be a doctor. Like your mum.

She's a nurse.

Slurp. Coulda been a doctor, is what I mean.

Why wasn't she?

Well, *gulp*, gid tea, that. There was no money for to go to university, son. Not like here. Back home, it was only the richies. Off to St. Andrew's and Cambridge, and see you, McKnight, get yourself a trade, boy. Nae chance. In the mines I was, by sixteen. Six-*teen*. With your mother it was nursing. But you could go to university, and know more than half the bampots in it do by the time you get there. I mean, look at this. Dad thumbs open *The Anatomy Coloring Book*. Look, he says, at the *detail* of this thing.

Jacob double-takes, bends closer. A big black-and-white eyeball glares back at him.

Dad pins down the page with his fingers, points to the muscles attached to the eye. Look here, son. The idea, see, is that you colour in each part differently – B, say, in green or what have you – then you use the same colour for the proper names of the parts on the left here, so's you remember. See? B, Inferior Rectus. You'd colour it –

Green, says Jacob, Inferior Rectus. But he can't look back at that eye.

Son, you can do this nae problem like, and then, what with how you can draw 'n' all, you should actually reproduce the drawings yourself, like medical students do with their dissections 'n' what have you. Dad draws his index finger down Jacob's torso, says Then you'd really know what you're made of.

Jacob eyes the long crevasse in his PJ top.

The whole human body you could know before you even get to high school. You'll breeze through, boyo, I'm tellin you.

Jacob just nods.

Dad claps his hands and slaps his thighs to make galloping sounds. Got tae get myself shaved and away, he says.

Thanks for the book, Dad.

Welcome.

Dad jumps up, heads off. Jacob just sits, looks at his face in the surface of the gold ball that Dad put back on the tree. He flicks it with his middle finger.

Tink.

Harder.

Tink.

Harder.

Tink!

But it doesn't break or fall.

Jacob eyes the book. Wrinkles his nose. Eyes the book. Looks out the window. Eyes the book. Thumbs pages.

Ankle bones.

The spleen.

Half a face, with the skin peeled off.

Jacob stops. Stares at a blank space on the wall.

Smells the Mennen Musk just before Dad says Son. Blinks hard and gives his head a shake and there's Dad. Uniform on. Speck of styptic on his top lip.

That you away, Dad?

Eh, not just yet. Good thing, too. The old boy was a bit late this year.

Huh?

There I am, shavin away, and look who's at the window. Cut meself. Sorry, he says to me and hands me this.

In Dad's hand is a big present. Shiny green paper. Perfect red bow.

Here you go, kid.

Jacob just looks at it. To: Jacob. From: St. Nicholas. Dad's handwriting.

What you waitin on, Christmas?

Jacob tugs the bow. Then rips the paper with both hands. A sketchbook! And Prismacolor pencils! Set of *sixty*!

Dad gets down on one knee, pats the back of Jacob's neck. Their foreheads kiss.

Merry Christmas, son.

Holy jumpin Merry Christmas, Dad! Wish I got something else for you.

Don't you worry 'bout that. But see you put they pencils to the use they're meant for.

Jacob nods and nods. I'm gonna colour all day.

You'll no be seeing the Hollingsworths at all?

Nope, says Jacob, picturing himself over there watching while Graham and Bobby show off all their presents. No way, he says.

Right then, says Dad, there's Chunky Soup in the cupboard, wee bit o' bread left. Should do you for lunch.

You on first turkey shift this year?

Will be whether they like it or no.

Five o'clock then?

Yepsir. Don't be late or we'll miss the mincemeat pie.

Okey-doke.

Okay then, I'm offskee. Gather up that paper, now.

Jacob listens to Dad thump down the stairs. Whacks back the curtains of the living room window, watches Dad brush snow off the Torino, back it out, and off he goes, fishtailing through fresh snow that sparkles under the streetlights.

What a good Christmas.

Jacob sticks his tummy out, and in his best Pavarotti voice he sings Tanka-YOO, and props the cassette beneath the tree and scoops up the wrapping paper. Makes a big ball and slams it on top of the spaghetti scraps. Flicks the cupboard door closed, steps right foot over left and disco spins to the fridge. Slugs back orange juice straight out the bottle. And spills it down his pyjamas when the phone rings. He watches it for another ring. Another.

... M'lo?

Ain't you up yet ... sucka?

Hey, Cracker.

What did you get?

What did *you* get?

GI Joe, Kung Fu Grip –

Neat.

New pair o' skates. And Evel Knievel. His car crashes. Has a parachute.

I saw it on TV.

You should come over, brotha. Guess what my dad got?

What.

Brand-new Ski-Doo. Rips. Him and Spielman's old man are taking us for rides.

Think I'll just stay in. Play with my new stuff.

So what did you get?

Prismacolor pencils, set of sixty. Best kind. Huge big sketchbook, too. And *The Anatomy Coloring Book.*

Colouring book?

Anatomy colouring book. You colour the body. The inside. It's dyno-mite.

Should come skidooing.

Maybe tomorrow.

Goin to Peterborough. Boxing Day.

Next day.

Maybe.

'Kay.

See ya, honky.

Jacob leaves the phone off the hook. Last year, Mum cried. And Dad grabbed the phone and said like a hiss *Lissen* to you, you daft bitch, into it on Christmas bloody mornin.

It's just postcards now, with pictures of grizzly bears, or High River, but if Dad sees them first they get torn up and Jacob has to sneak the pieces out the garbage, put them back together.

– ark is very beautiful –

– ill love you and your fath –

Hard to square how she sounds in her writing now with back then. Screaming and teeth and nails. The ashtray *zing* by Jacob's ear and *smash* against the wall. Are you out of your head, woman? I do no want this anymore. Then get the fuck gone with you – you hear me? – get the fuck gone with you.

> *Dear Mum,*
> *How are you? I am fine.*

That's as far as Jacob gets usually. Son, have you any idea the size of the hole your mother left us in? Have you? And that's what the paper looks like when Jacob tries a letter – a hole, and words just disappear down it.

But he turns to where he thinks west is and says Merry Christmas, Mum, from your son, Jacob.

After a lie-down Jacob wedges his pillow in the corner, sits with the sketchbook, the colouring book and the pencils stacked in his lap. Pops the clasp of the pencil case, slowly pushes the lid open.

Holy jumpin. *Look* at them all.

Blendable, water soluble, says the leaflet. Unique pure pigments. Ideal for the professional artist.

Jacob takes out a few pencils, twirls them between his fingers, holds them up to his nose. Whispers names of colours. Viridian Green. Cobalt Teal. Burnt Sienna. He wants to draw – Iron Man, crimson, gold, invincible. Cyclops and his crackling radioactive eyes. But then he remembers Dad's eyes – See you put them to the use they're made for – and sets the sketchbook aside. Tells himself he'll colour one, just one bit. Heart starting to thump, he opens the book. Sees, eyes wide, a mouth spread like *Hustler* legs, with clips holding back the lips, baring the teeth and gums. The tongue, it looks alive.

Jacob swallows, turns pages. Cells. Muscle fibres. Nerves. The pelvic girdle.

A boy.

Half a boy. Dissected. His mouth, hanging open. *Child*, says the caption under him, *of Uncertain Years*. But he looks about eight or nine. And has the exact same hair.

Jacob looks away and says It's just a picture. But he crawls into bed, curls like a busted C.

P_{age} a day, that's the best way to go, slow but steady like a long run. That way the bits and blanks stay away, and Jacob can get to the housework, too. Fridge needs defrosting, dishes need done, tub wants a scrubbing, and the oven. The oven. Dad always burns meat pies and bangers. So Jacob scrubs and washes and, in between, he colours. The spine in shining silver, the elbow in a grey like steel. Then, on the morning before 1979, when Jacob is finishing the muscles of facial expression, it snows like bonkers and Cracker calls.

Hospital Hill, sucka!

Tobogganing?

It will be dyno-mite.

Don't got a toboggan, remember?

You be borrowin mine.

I dunno. Might stay in.

You colouring again?

And drawing.

Colouring ... and drawing, colouring ... and drawing.

Have to.

Why?

Just have to.

Just come.

'Kay. I'll come.

But Jacob, still in his PJS, goes back to his room and the muscles of facial expression. Use warm and cheerful colours, say the instructions, for the muscles (A–H) producing a smile. Colour the muscles reflecting sadness (I–O) with greens, blues and greys. Begin with the smiling side. Repeat the process with the sad side.

Jacob picks Neutral Grey from his Prismacolors, begins to colour L, Depressor Anguli Oris, on the sad side. But switches to the smiling side and colours D, Levator Labii Superioris. Labia means lips on your mouth or a woman's vulva. The right eye in this picture is so sad. And the guy who drew it, Jacob thinks, must be a real artist, not a scientist, because more than how a muscle moves makes an eye look sad like that.

He pushes the book away. Pictures Dean Spielman's face. How he twists his mouth. The way, without speaking, he can say So where's *your* Krazy Karpet? Friends sometimes are better than being alone, but sometimes you're complete bastards to each other, too. Like Spielman. Not sure you like him but afraid not to pretend to because he might beat the crap out of you.

Jacob looks at his watch. It's after three. Was supposed to stick in a quick two-miler today. But he can sprint up Hospital Hill after each run down, meet Dad when he gets off and say he did intervals. Maybe go down to the Riverbend for a hot chocolate. Depending on Dad's day.

He huffs it to the hospital, sees the Gran Torino in the parking lot as he walks over to the hill. The guys are at the top. Fighting.

I'm not doin' it, says Dean. *You* do it.

Screw you, honky, says Cracker. *You* do it.

They both look at Bobby, who's sucking on the end of his mitten. The pompom on his toque wobbles as he shakes his head and stomps around and glues every word together. Un-unh-no-way-nope-always-me.

Chickennn, says Dean.

Know-y'are-but-what-am-I?

Are you even speaking English?

Then Bobby sees Jacob. Points. McKnight! McKnight-said-he'd-do-it! He said!

And everybody looks at Jacob.

Little bugger, Jacob says to himself. But he did tell Bobby he'd do it. Only Bobby. Everybody says they'll do it sometime. Jacob just told Bobby because of last winter. So Bobby wouldn't get hurt again.

But Dean starts chanting. Do *it*, do *it*, and Cracker and Bobby – pricks – join in.

Jacob, snow in his eyes, looks down Hospital Hill at the edge of the Wall.

That's what everybody calls it, the big retaining wall built into the steepest part of Hospital Hill, about halfway up. Except for Dead Man's behind the factory, Hospital Hill is the steepest. Starts at the edge of Glanisberg Memorial's parking lot and *phoom* goes all the way to the high school football field. Usually you toboggan well to the Wall's left. Usually have to, or you'll slide *smack* into the Wall's backside. But on blowy days like today the snow drifts right up to the edge, and someone, probably Spielman, has packed snow against it. A perfect ramp.

Dooo *it*, dooo *it*.

Jacob thinks of crazy Shawn Quinn, who bit a guy, and of his little brother, Terry, except everyone calls him Bulldog. In summer they pour out half a jug of Becker's Jungle Juice, fill it with vodka. Slug it back and do meatballs off the Black Bridge. Shawn throws his dog in first. Complete bampots, says Dad. But not even the Quinns have jumped the Wall.

DO it do it do it. DO it do it do it.

Stop!

Do IT, do IT, do IT!

Jacob stares at Bobby. His eyes like beggars, *Please, Jacob, not me.* Bobby'll do almost anything to stay in the group. Smack a cow on the ass, pee on Mr. McCluskey's petunias, chuck chestnuts at Fish and Chippers' hot rods. But not this. Last winter was the biggest ramp ever. Old tires and hay bales, plywood and packed snow. Dean told Bobby it was a test, and Cracker, the chicken, wouldn't even stand up for his brother. Bobby almost cried. Had to use his puffer but *thump* dove headfirst down the hill. Hit the ramp like a boat on a huge big wave. Toboggan this way, Bobby that way. *Crunch.* Everybody slid down on their bums and Bobby slapped the snow *I can't mooovvve!* Dean looked *Do* something, and Jacob ran hard up the hill and right into the ambulance office. Dad Dad come quick Bobby wiped out and he might be quadra-phoenic! Just a hairline fracture of the coccyx, but Molly Hollings-worth brought the X-ray to the waiting room. Pick on someone your own size, ya buncha goons! In spring, they all had a laugh about it, *quadraphoenic*, though it wasn't that funny.

Do it, do it, do ...

He's not gonna do it, says Spielman.

Bobby starts to bolt, but Spielman just flops down. Starts – *swoosh-swa* – making an angel and says *Chick*-en, *chick*-en, McKnight's a big *chick*-en.

Bobby's eyes say Jacob you don't have to you don't.

Cracker just stares at the ground, tongue curled under his nose.

Hollingsworth, says Jacob, stop licking your snot.

Dean stops swooshing and looks up and says Yeah, snot licker. But then he starts in again, Chick-en – *swoosh-swa* – McKnight's a big chicken – *swoosh-swa*.

Jacob eyeballs Dean's flashy coat and ski pants. Starts walking to the hospital.

Dean says *Knew* it, just when Dad comes out the ambulance office doors, waving See ya, lads, over his shoulder.

And Jacob spins.

Runs right at Dean. Grabs his Krazy Karpet and dives.

Behind him Cracker yells Crazy mutha! Jump off, Jacob!

But Jacob aims for the ramp dead on, and holy shit he is *moving*. Snow spits in his face. Eyes closed, bits and pieces slamming against their backsides – bone and bloody mess and the ashtray smashing and there's the Wall coming at him like a fist *fwoop*, he's up, and over.

Sky in his eyes.

But it falls away from him and then a sound like a hockey stick *snap* over a knee, but Jacob knows it's bone. He curls, clenches his toes. Rolls. And sits up, his head leaning all on its own way over Jacob's left shoulder.

Up top Cracker and Bobby are screaming Mr. McKnight Mr. McKnight!

But Dad just waits, pops a Fisherman's Friend in his mouth, puts his hands in his parka pockets as Jacob, holding his arm by the elbow, climbs. When he gets to the top, Dad says Think you can fly?

Jacob tries to shrug.

And Dad bites down on the lozenge, nods his head toward the hospital. Let's go then.

Dean doesn't look at them as they walk by, just keeps kneeling in the stepped-on angel.

Jacob's not sure what was in that shot, but it was a humdinger. His tongue feels fat and sleepy, but he manages to ask if he can see the X-rays. Mrs. Hollingsworth looks at Dad. He nods, grumbles as he ducks through the curtains. He told Mrs. H and Dr. Smythe no X-rays, any fool can see the boy's bust his collarbone. Patch him up meself, Chrissakes. Mrs. H told him not to talk nonsense, they've got to see what kind of break in case it needs pins. *Pins?* She probably doesn't know that Dad isn't Canadian yet, he's a Landed Immigrant and just a part-timer. No OHIP. And Jacob wonders how you figure what a collarbone's worth when Mrs. H pops her head in and asks how's he feeling.

Tickety-boo.

Pain?

Don't feel a thing.

Mrs. Hollingsworth ruffles his hair and ducks out.

Jacob sits up, slides to the edge of the gurney. Blinks. Other side of the curtains Mrs. Hollingsworth says Poor thing, and laughs. Dad growls and grumbles, but Mrs. H says Oh shoosh, not to worry, it'll be taken care of. Then she comes back in and *p-tunk, p-tunk* puts up two X-rays on the display board, flicks a switch. There you be, Jacob.

That's me?

That's you.

Jacob looks at his bones. They have haloes. He blinks, focuses. Vertebrae. Sternum. Floating rib. Humerus.

Very good, Jacob.

The ulnar nerve goes along here.

Is that a fact.

Jacob nods, tells Mrs. Hollingsworth that *The Anatomy Coloring Book* says when you press the ulnar nerve hard enough, it speaks. That's what it says in the book. Nerves speak. Jacob asks if Mrs. H knows what sort of thing the ulnar nerve might have to say, and would you be able to understand it.

Aren't those painkillers fun, dear?

Mrs. H pats Jacob on the head, ducks back out the curtains. Tells Dad and a nurse about the things Jacob just said, and the nurse has a laugh. Dad doesn't.

Then Dr. Smythe and his aftershave come through the curtains like a breeze, and his crisp white coat swishes, and he has an accent like Mum's.

A-llo, Jacob.

'Lo.

'Ad a nawsty fawl, did we?

Jacob shrugs with his good shoulder.

Right then, let's have a look.

Jacob smiles at Dr. Smythe's voice and his Mentos breath. The mint clicks across his teeth as he palpates with soft, clean fingers.

Pain here, Jacob? says Dr. Smythe, pressing near Jacob's nipple.

Jacob nods.

Bad?

One-shouldered shrug.

You've probably also torn your pectoral muscle, says Dr. Smythe, turning to the X-ray. Jacob looks at his nipple. When he was little he thought it was called a pupil and Dad said No, son, tits are blind.

Not often I hear laughs in here, says Dr. Smythe.

Best medicine, says Jacob.

Quite. Well. Heah, Jacob, says the Doc, tip of pen *tap tap* on the X-ray. See that, Jacob? You've fractured your *clah*-vicle.

Jacob stares at the ends of bone, one on top of the other. He touches ever so lightly the lump under his skin as Dr. Smythe flicks a switch and the bones lose their glow.

You're being a very bryve boy, I must say, Jacob.

Jacob blinks, heavy eyes.

Hmm. Well. Let's get you mended. Be right back.

Dr. Smythe disappears through the curtains. And Jacob lies back, remembers what it felt like, for those few seconds, flying.

But at home that night Dad hulks. *Thuds* his palm against his temple and says What gets into that fucking *head* of yours? Eh? *Thud, thud.*

Jacob stares at the coffee table. Tries not to breathe. It hurts.

Eh?

Jacob stares.

I'm *talkin* to you.

Jacob meets his eyes.

That's you for four bloody weeks, Dad says, holding four fingers in Jacob's face. At least four weeks. Six with the physio you'll be needin. *That* we will do *here*, Dad says, standing straight, hands on hips as he paces. *I* will show you the exercises you need to do.

Jacob keeps his eyes on Dad as he paces, paces. Under his breath he says two hundred and fifty fucking *dollars*, then turns away and thumps to the kitchen, where he whacks open cupboards and clangs and bashes pots and pans on the stove. Four weeks, he says, and you just increasing your distance.

Jacob tells himself he's glad he broke his shitstinking collarbone. No cold black mornings. No wind. No hills. But as he watches Dad get the supper on, snot slides out his nose. He snuffs it up and says Sorry, Dad.

Dad lifts the pan this way that way to spread the Crisco and says G'wan to your room. I'll call you when it's ready.

In his bedroom Jacob gets down – slow – on one knee, feels under his bed. Slides his sketchbook and pencils out. Opens one-handed the pencil case's clasp. The case convulses and pencils pop out. He picks up the sketching pencil with his other hand. Blinks through pain as he tries to draw a clavicle. But with his right hand he can barely hold the pencil proper. Flings it across the room. Fingers *The Anatomy Coloring Book* from the shelf under his night-stand and flips through the skeletal system to Plate 28. Looks for a colour. Picks Payne's Grey. Tries.

But stops colouring – Fuck this hurts – when he goes outside the lines.

Boy.

Yeah?

Doesn't take two hands to set a table.

Coming.

In the kitchen Dad squints and stands way back from the hissing spitting pan. He's got the heat on way too high again. The bangers split and ooze like wounds.

When school's back in, word gets round fast. Jacob *McKnight*? Tried the *Wall*? Bulldog Quinn brings over his pack of Little Bastards at recess, spits and says You got guts, man. And Gimpy-Gail McBride even wants to see it.

What?

Your bone.

Jacob hooks his thumb in his sweater, pulls.

Gross. Hurt?

Not much.

Liar.

Gail would know. She's had a gimpy leg ever since she was born. People say it was the way she was in the womb plus the doctor was bombed and just gave her a yank. She had an operation, but can't have another one till she's done growing. Used to get teased. Still does, but now it's because of her boobs. It's like God said Sorry, Gail, for the bum leg, and *boom* gave her huge big boobs in one summer. Bulldog and the Little Bastards pull her bra strap, cop feels. Gail gives them hell, but can't chase them. And Jacob can't think of anything to say when Gail keeps standing there, blinking behind her glasses and giving him – Jacob swallows – a look of *double entendre*.

Well, she says, *bye*. And limpy-gimps off.

Jacob has a quick look at her bum. It's like two hams, Gail's bum. Plus he would like to kiss her Mound of Venus. But knows he's chicken. So tonight it's pulling-the-goalie time, with the wrong hand. That's what Spielman calls it, pulling the goalie, except Spielman says he doesn't need to anymore, he gets real hand jobs from girls like Melissa Fowler who smoke and pay Jacob no attention at all. But you can tell Spielman is still a bit jealous over all the attention Jacob is getting. And still a little sorry, too – Jacob could have broken his back, not his collarbone. Another reason that Dad's still acting Payne's Grey. In class Jacob tries to pay attention but especially in math he drifts like a cloud and remembers the *snap* – could have been your neck, you daft shit – and pictures Dad in his Black Watch kilt again, whisky splashing out his glass when he says It's not proper, a father outlive his lad, fucksakes.

When Miss Richardson first sees the sling, she shakes her head and her shiny earrings wobble, but she can't stop her orbicularis oculi and her zygomaticus major from activating. Smiles like dawn. How's the arm, Captain Marvel?

Fractured my clavicle, Miss R. Can't draw.

Can't do a lot of things, I imagine.

That smirk of hers. A real whiplasher. You can never tell if Miss Richardson is doing the old *double entendre* either. Jacob wonders if she knows that he pulls the goalie imagining her sometimes. Miss R's a scorcher. But even though Jacob shares jokes with Spielman and Cracker about her honkers and Mr. Kazinski feeding her the big one in the back of his ranch wagon, Jacob doesn't like to, and his face heats like an element whenever Miss R smirks like that and makes ambiguous statements. Or maybe, Jacob thinks, I just hear *double entendres* and I am daft and horny. Best play it cool. So when Miss R asks, Jacob tells her that he has no Special Needs. I'm tickety-boo, Miss R, hunky-dory.

Sure?

Yeah, look. Jacob shows her how he can still write with his arm in the sling. He folds a sheet of paper in half, and, pinching the bottom corner with his other hand, tugs it bit by bit as he prints.

Jacob, that's ridiculous. I can make arrange–

No. It's okay.

Their eyes lock.

Really, says Jacob, it's no big whoop.

Honey, you must be in pain.

Jacob nods, but says I'm on analgesics. They can cause drowsiness, but overall they do not impede –

Okay, okay, suit yourself.

Back to fractions, Jacob says, pointing tallyho with his left arm, then wincing. The pills don't always work that well.

Miss Richardson's voice is like jelly rolls and custard and can make even fractions feel good, but math is still crap. Universal language, my butt, Jacob says to himself. Spielman is actually pretty good at it, and could probably get just as good marks as the girls in the class if he applied himself. Jacob wishes he would. Then Spielman wouldn't feel so dumb in other classes and have to play the hard man in the playground. Everybody should be good in at least one subject. One real subject. Spielman's good just in gym. Jacob's pretty good at just about anything except for math. Dad crumpled up his last report card and threw it against the wall and said How in fuck are you going to be a doctor with arithmetic grades like that? He stomped and he paced but couldn't stay steamed for long. He's shit at math, too. Still counts on his fingers. But knows sort of what's needed for a good life, so you don't have to up and leave your home, fucksakes, sloggin it out in mines till you're on your own two feet.

Jacob tries to contract his brain like a muscle, focus, but Miss R starts to speak like it's a foreign language, and his head bobs, nods, bounces. Nods, bobs, bounces. Miss R gives homework. Says You'd all better get started on it now, and sits down at her desk.

Jacob stares at the page. Blinks. Stares. Then Dean whispers his name. Jacob looks over and Dean hides his mouth with his hand, says You can copy mine if you want.

As the days wear on, Jacob does everything he can just to stay awake in class, never mind take notes. Nights, flat on his back, he breathes deep and with each breath imagines a brush loaded with gold or silver paint – over and back, over and back it goes in long smooth strokes, painting the ends of the fracture together. But sometimes it gives him a boner, too. He tries to give it a pull – O Gail, you have become so lovely – but with his right hand it doesn't feel half as good. Why does one half of your body not do what you tell it? Imagine if you could write with both hands, and write about different things, too. Math with one hand, English with the other. Or you could do homework and have a pull at the same time.

Shut your filthy ...

That was Dad, at them again. The night hisses. Jacob's heard them before, but never knew until lying awake half the night every night just how often they happen. Sometimes his heart pounds, hearing them – your filthy *mouth*, cunt – and it's hard to breathe. Dad sounds like he could kill someone, but he never wakes up, and he just says You're hearing things, when Jacob asks who he was talking to last night.

Then one morning near the end of January Jacob's eyes blink open, and he remembers no night hisses. No sudden stabs or dull slow aches. And his arm is halfway out the sling.

Holy jumpin, I slept!

Over supper that night Jacob tells Dad maybe he's ready to hit the road again. When I walk I don't feel a thing, honest.

Without looking up as he chews his liver Dad says Since when is walking running?

Jacob shrugs his right shoulder and says See that?

You'll still be healing yet, says Dad, be patient.

Been almost four weeks, Dad.

Rest, son. Rest.

But later that week Dad draws up a personalized rehabilitation program, writes the exercises and the number of repetitions to be done on the calendar. Begin with walking your hand up the wall. Followed by arm bends. Then weighted arm bends. Soup can at first, then the little sandbags Dad borrows from the physio lab. Build up to curls and extensions, three sets of each. Muscles around breaks have been traumatized and tend to atrophy. Need restrengthening. Except for serious tears or trauma, you can get a muscle right back up to one hundred per cent. The body, says Dad, is a remarkable thing. And the ends of his collarbone, Jacob can feel it, they clasp like a good strong handshake, and Jacob goes back to helping out with wee jobs, mostly one-armers. Cleaning the toilet and the washroom sink, taking out the garbage. He figures out how to spin the bag with his hand and foot, then get the twist tie on before it unravels.

See that, Dad?

Aren't you a marvel.

Sometimes when Dad looks at the sling it's like he's forgotten all about it, but then he remembers and his face folds and furrows. Except for the night hisses, though, he's getting on okay. Even makes the tea before *M*A*S*H* or *Monday Night Football*. Imitates Howard Cosell and gives Jacob anatomy quizzes during commercials. How many valves has the heart, and what are their names?

Jacob chews his ginger crisp and says Four: tricuspid, pulmonary, mitral and aortic.

Bang on, Doc.

Jacob reads a lot about the heart these days. Its beat is controlled by the sino-atrial node, which is a real pacemaker, not the fake ones they have to put in if your SA node is dysfunctional. Imagine, Jacob thinks, if you could invent a brain pacemaker. It would take a genius like Tony Stark to make something like that. People could have a good laugh, the best medicine, more often. Especially Dad, because he can turn on a dime. One night, just after laughing all through *M*A*S*H*, they're watching a documentary on JFK and Jacob says How 'bout a quiz, Dad? and Dad slashes the air with his hand and says *Shut* it.

They've seen shows like this a lot, and Jacob has to sit there and listen to Dad's theories. It was fucken CIA, boy, in cahoots with the Mob and Castro. This time is no different, Dad is glued to the screen. Taps it *tink tink* as they slow-mo the film so much that you can see JFK's brains spill like Chunky Soup into his wife's lap. There, says Dad, when the president's head whiplashes, you're telling me that shot's comin from behind?

They say it's recoil, Dad.

No fucken way, kid. I've fired a rifle, seen what it can do. Trust me, boyo. That shot is from straight on, look, look at the brains and blood and bits of bone that spray over the boot of the car? Jesus. Dad falls back on the sofa, sips his Golden. Dour. A shameful day that was, son. Shameful. Him and his brother both, the bastards got.

Jacob feels sorry sometimes for JFK and for Jackie O with the blood on her dress but why does Dad when he was living in Scotland the day JFK got shot? One time he spent ages looking at photos in a special *Playboy* about presidential assassinations, and he even made drawings on graph paper. Vectors. Angles of inflection. Came up with a Plan, and the masterminds. Jack Ruby was the patsy, he says. Bloody decoy. We're talking about American agencies, son, kill their own leaders. Fucken hell.

It's good, Jacob thinks, to be groan up in Canada. Scottish guys like Dad go on and on about Caribbean immigrants and Culloden and JFK and Marilyn Monroe. And they get sad so fast. Dad's got enough to be sad about. A brain pacemaker would be one of the best inventions ever.

But the morning after the JFK documentary, Dad's forgotten all about a second gunman and the CIA, and kneels in front of Jacob. Sling off, shirt off. Arm feels like it was stuck on in place of his real one, and he has to think about keeping it straight or else it folds like a wing over his chest. Crook of his elbow feels like it's made of tire, and the upper arm is thinner than his right one. But no pain. Just a little lump like a robin's egg where the break calcified.

Jacob closes his eyes as Dad's big thick thumb palpates around the lump, brushes over it, then presses on it. Jacob winces, but it doesn't hurt, it just feels soft, and new.

Dad's halitosis is bad today, but he's scrubbed his hands like a doctor and they smell like Ivory. Dr. Smythe said follow-up X-rays might be a good idea considering the nature of the break, but Dad says his hands know bone. He'll tell ol' Doc how it's healed.

And his fingertips feel a little cold, but Dad's hands are cradles. Dad's hands have held babies wet with womby goo. Dad's hands have brought hearts back. Dad's hands tried so hard – *One* and *two* and – but Jacob blinks the bits away because Dad isn't remembering that now. Look at him smile when he says Cat's arse, kid, this has healed beautifully.

Really?

Boyo, believe me, you are ready to *run*.

But at first the runs are real slogs. Get that *head* up, boy. Takes about a week for Jacob just to get his breathing back, but Dad keeps the distances down, the pace slow. No hill work. And at least the mornings aren't quite so black, quite so cold. Over the days – That's more like it, boy – Jacob's form comes back, and the pace picks up. His colouring, too. Like using a whole new hand at first. Making messes. Outside the lines. Have to keep practicing. Spleen. The lymphoid system. For immunity. And by the middle of March it's right back to the distances they were doing before the Wall, and a page a day, too, when *ping* he shows up. The New Kid. Like he stepped out of a hole in the air. Alvy. Alvy Chatwin. Funny name. Funny-looking, too. Little, like he's in Grade Four, not Seven. White hair almost. Glasses. And the scar. That's what everyone calls him: the kid with the scar. Hard not to stare at it – goes from his ear to his chin, along the jaw – when Jacob watches him, every day, just sitting there all by himself in the corner of the cafeteria. Sipping chocolate milk through a skinny straw. And drawing.

Kids point and snicker and whisper, but it's like he's in a cocoon all his own and the whispers and snickers bounce off. Spielman wants to know what the guy's problem is and Cracker says he's no dumbass, that's for sure. Answers everything in science. Does math in his head. Doesn't do shit in gym, Spielman says, and takes Cracker's big chicken sandwich.

That's mine, honky.

Trade.

Peanut butter?

Trade.

Jacob gets up. Starts going over there. Ignores Spielman when he says You want half of this? Gimpy-Gail giggles with her friends when Jacob comes closer, but they stop and one says *Nerd* when Jacob keeps on going.

Hi.

Hi.

Whatcha drawing?

Soon as Jacob asks he pictures himself jumping and hunching and covering the page. But this Alvy guy, he just looks up, blinks and says *Wolverine* like it's any other word. And before he speaks another, Jacob knows. You just know. And Alvy's sketch. The motion. The detail in the forearm.

Holy jumpin, says Jacob, that's *good*.

Thanks. Gobstopper?

Jacob feels Cracker's stare – and Spielman's stare – and he thinks about his cavity, too, but he says Sure, and – Alvy shoves down – has a seat. Holds out his hand. Alvy shakes the box once, twice.

Two? says Jacob.

Alvy points at each cheek, says One on each side.

With Dad working nights these days and getting home knackered in the morning it's Jacob down the Sterling Road alone after school. Lots of time to think about inside anatomy and Alvy plus anything you like. No Dad, no bits, no pieces. No blanks. Just road. And cows. They come right up to the fences and watch Jacob go by. Funny. Running can be okay when you're alone. Helps you do a philosophy, which comes from Greek for *loving wisdom*. Dad showed Jacob *Hume, David* in the *Wee Book of Famous Scots* about unmatched contributions to the creative tapestry of man. Said the Scots-Irish mind is distinguished, but a little knowledge is a dangerous thing, boy. Maybe he's right because look at the old guy in the Rembrandt book that Dr. Henderson left at the library. *Philosopher Reading.* A fat leather book the size of the Toronto Yellow Pages. Old guy's face looks like he's trying to let out a huge big fart stuck inside him. Out here, Jacob thinks, just chugging along, ideas pop up like calcium supplement. Effervescence. Get this *in* you, boy. Bones take an awful pounding out there. *Fzzz.* The body needs supplements.

Jacob hits the halfway mark. Turns. Takes it easy. Feels the sun on his face. Snow's almost all gone. And it can be so strong, too, the body, because what else can go for a few miles on a ham sandwich and a glass of milk? You'd be richer than the guy who owns the chocolate factory if you invented a car that could run on milk. Air'd be better, too, but if cars had digestive systems like people then they would flatulate (which comes from the Latin for *to blow*) instead of making exhaust, and what with the number of cars on the roads can you imagine that. Plus if a car blows one tire or one valve then that's it buggered. But look at the body. Lose an eye, or a kidney fails, or a lung collapses, and you can still get by.

More vital organs should come in twos.

Would a kidney miss its twin? And would all the extra work it has to do make it die sooner than normal?

Jacob shakes his head, breathes out *phooh*. Keep your mind on what you're doon, boy. Here comes the gate to the park already, just a coupla miles to go and –

No.

The Gran Torino, parked in there where the cop cars hide. And Dad, leaning on the hood. His face.

Jacob corrects his form, picks up the pace, but it's too late.

I knew it! I fuckingwell knew it. You're doggin it, boy. When I'm no here you're doggin it.

No, Dad, I –

Shoulders square! Back straight! Knees *up*. And *get* bloody goan. You're training for *races*, not a walk in the park.

Sorry.

Move.

Dad gets in the Gran Torino and roars off. On the seat beside him, Jacob knows, is the ticking stopwatch. Dad'll drive ahead exactly a mile, stop the car and watch every second.

Anything over six minutes and I'm dead, Jacob says.

Then he blows hard out both nostrils and *goes.*

Phooh, hah.

Phooh, hah.

A mile later his lungs feel like lava, but he blows right by Dad when he stops the watch.

Where you goan?

Jacob pumps his arms.

Rein it in.

Jacob keeps going. All breath and burn and motion.

But outside Hillcrest Heights he gets a bang on the ear for going too hard. Across the street Teddy goes nuts, pulls at his chain.

Shut it! Coulda pulled a muscle, bampot.

Jacob gets his breath back. My time, he says.

Eh?

The split. What was my time?

Shut it, you unholy mutt! Five forty-eight, big shot.

Best ever.

Yeah, no bad. Inside. Shower.

Jacob hangs his head, but on the way to the door he sneaks a wink at Teddy.

Just before March Break Cracks asks Jacob if he wants to go to the orchards after school and peg a few birds. McKnight can't come, says Spielman.

Says who? says Jacob.

Can't borrow *my* gun.

See if I care, Spielman.

You can use my gun, brotha.

Doesn't want to, says Spielman, wants to draw pictures with Scar Boy.

He had an *operation*, Dean, says Jacob. Mandibular readjustment. So he could swallow and talk better.

So what?

So you don't have to tease him about it.

Everybody else does.

It's true. Even girls. Hey, Alberta Boy, where's your cowboy hat? Hey, Scar Boy, where's your horse? Alvy acts like he's got bulletproof ears, but Jacob knows what it's like – getting looked at. Talked about. Why don't they just shut their garbage mouths?

I don't care, Jacob. They're evolutionary throwbacks.

You got guts, Alvy. And you talk great.

Toffee?

Alvy always brings candy. Especially when they draw together. At lunch. Or after school, when Jacob doesn't have to do speed work or get the supper on. Alvy uses Blue Line Brite White Comic Book Art Boards. Just like the pros. Draws all the big ones – Fantastic Four, Spiderman, Batman – but also invents super-heroes with their own origins and whole storylines and every-thing. Gemini, a mutant who can replicate herself and touch you into paralysis. Peregrine, who lives in a secret Rocky Mountain hideaway and dives down on bad guys and traps them in his tita-nium talons. One day at Becker's Jacob finally gets up the guts.

Alvy?

Yeah?

Where in Alberta did you live?

Kind of all over. Mostly Red Deer.

What's it like there?

Kind of a shithole. Sort of better than here, though.

I might wanna go sometime.

To Red Deer?

High River.

Joe Clark lives there.

So does my mum.

Oh. Alvy goes quiet for a sec. Then he pulls out some licorice. Bite?

Sure. Jacob chews, says Let's do a Peregrine story today.

'Kay. Public library.

Alvy always wants to go there, even though they get looks from Mrs. Bailey for talking or for looking at Picasso and Dali pictures in the books Dr. Trudy Henderson left. When they're done, Jacob always goes this way, Alvy that way. And you can tell. He doesn't want you to come. But Jacob keeps his mouth shut. Nobody comes over to his place either. And Jacob doesn't want anyone coming over. So he feels guilty when he doubles back one day and follows Alvy. Because it's Booth Street. Near the factory. In one of the houses that look like skin disease. Same kind of place Dad and him lived in just after Mum left. Jacob waits till Alvy goes in, turns. And runs hard. But he has to slow down, walk. Breathing's all off. Cracker and Bobby and Spielman have huge big houses and anything they want, five bucks a week allowance and they don't even care. Don't even share their candy.

So on the day before the clocks go forward when Cracker calls and says Comin to the factory? Jacob says No, Alvy and I are drawing. They're supposed to work on Gemini, but just eat chocolate bars and goof off the whole afternoon. Draw Picasso penises right on the table, with smiley faces in the glans. Jacob laughs because of how Alvy laughs, no sound but his whole little body has an earthquake and his glasses slide down his nose. Mrs. Bailey thumps around and whams books back on the shelves and says down the stairs *Quiet.*

Sorry, Mrs. B.

That's Mrs. Bailey, Jacob McKnight. And here she comes *clomp clomp.*

Alvy erases like crazy. Leans on his elbow to cover the last penis just when Mrs. Bailey pokes her head round the corner. Jacob, you used to come here and read quietly. Not drawing comics and making noise.

But there's no one here, Mrs. Bailey.

I'm here, she says, and then she looks at Alvy like her life is his fault.

Let's just go, Jacob.

Wonderful idea, young man, and take your candy wrappers with you. Catch you eating in here again and I'll tear up your card.

Tear up this, you old bag, Alvy says soon as they're outside, and he pokes his butt at the door and lets one fly. They run and laugh but it's the same soon as they hit Bridge Street hill. All the way up Alvy stays quiet, keeps his head down. Works his gobstopper from one cheek to the other. Jacob's heart thumps when they get close to the corner of Bridge and Booth, but he says, natural-like, Me and my dad used to live down that way.

Alvy stays quiet.

Can show you, says Jacob. Liked it there.

Alvy doesn't say okay, but he doesn't say no, either. So Jacob follows, a bit behind. Until Alvy says Come on, poky. Peregrine grip! says Jacob, and he claw-holds Alvy's ribs. Runs ahead.

And Alvy chases him. Then stops hard.

Jacob looks up the street. What's the matter?

It's my mom.

What's she doing?

Gardening.

My mum liked gardening.

But it's like Alvy doesn't even hear. Moves his gobstopper this side, that side, is just about to talk when Hey! the woman yells up the street. Then she puts her thumb and finger in her mouth and whistles louder than Spielman can, and waves Come on o-ver.

I can go, says Jacob, pointing up Church.

Think it's okay. C'mon.

But when they get closer, Alvy's face goes stiff. His mum's on her hands and knees, bum stuck way up, turning over dirt with a little wee spade. Cigarette in her mouth like René Lévesque. And a tall plastic glass on the grass by her left ankle, leaning like the Tower of Pisa. Ice cubes. Lime. Gin. You can smell it from here. But Jacob blinks, puts a smile on his face.

Hey, boys, says Alvy's mum round her bouncy cigarette, how's it going?

Just when Jacob says Great, Mrs. Chatwin stands and *tak* knocks over her drink.

Shit and pigeons, she says.

And Alvy's shoulders hunch.

But Mrs. Chatwin just laughs like sand and wet gravel. Wipes her hands one against the other, sticks the right one out and says Hi, I'm Alvy's mom. Nice meetin ya.

I'm Jacob.

Figured. Alvy's told me all about you.

Really?

You're the runner.

Yup, me and my Dad.

Mrs. Chatwin *flik* sends her cig end over end into the dirt. Wanna come in? Alvy? What's up, kid?

Jacob has a quick look. Alvy's face. Tight. I should get going, Mrs. Chatwin.

Sure? We got extra pork chops. You like Payday?

Sorry?

Monopoly? Alvy loves games. Used to, anyway. Eh, Alv?

Maybe some other day, Mrs. Chatwin. I have to get home. Get the supper on. For my dad.

Alvy's mum says Oh.

And everything's quiet for a couple of secs, and the breeze lifts up her wispy hair and she smooths it over her ear.

Someday soon, though, says Jacob.

Any time, says Mrs. Chatwin, any time. Right, Alv?

Jacob whaps Alvy on the shoulder like to say It's all tickety-boo.

But Alvy barely says bye.

Wasn't that bad, Jacob tells himself on the way home. Pork chops. Payday. And just the way she said *Oh*. It was like the sound grew, and inside it you could see blended colours. Nice ones. Not Payne's Grey. Maybe a little. But sky-blue, too. And violet. Her liver maybe is a bit black, but you could colour her heart like lilacs. Alvy's face, it went half-dead. But he knows things. The things other people don't. Like with Dad. Neily Waldengarden and the nurses at the hospital cafeteria go on You do such a great job, Johnny, it must be so hard. And Dad just shrugs and says The bairn and I get by. Nurses and Neily don't know the night hisses. Don't see him out the Sterling Road. Dad's heart wouldn't even be Payne's Grey. It would be the same colour as iron. Like a safe. With another heart you can't see – violet, too, maybe, or light light yellow – inside it. Like Alvy's mum – little rough on the surface, like the old house, but her inside anatomy has lovely colours. You can tell. You can just tell.

TWO

Bright sunny day again and outside everything smells like sewers and mud. Spring. Everyone has their coats off. Girls skip. And even though the field's still a bit soggy, Spielman rounds up a bunch of guys for baseball at lunch. Even Alvy. Except he didn't bring his glove. Jacob says he has an extra one, kind of small but it should fit. He'll run home and grab it.

On his way over, Jacob sees bampot Chuck Linton across the street. Bottle of beer in his hand. Walking all wobbly across his crabgrassy lawn. Teddy *snap* hits the end of his chain, barks at him. Chuck just says Fuck off, fires up his old flatbed, pulls out. Teddy walks round and round in little circles, and whimpers.

Jacob whistles.

And Teddy lifts his tail like a question.

Hey, buddy, hang on a minute. Jacob shoots up the stairs. Roots through his closet.

There it is.

Along with the other pretend football helmet, the glove's the only thing Dad didn't take down to the Sally Ann. Just didn't see it, Jacob guesses. So small. But so's Alvy.

Five more minutes maybe before the game gets going. Just time for bologna and a quick hello. Been a while now since Jacob had a chance to sneak over.

Teddy stands stiff, stares, when Jacob crosses the road and steps, slow, slow, onto Linton's lawn.

Where is it? says Jacob in a nice-doggy voice, and he gets a little closer. Where's your bone? What did you do wid it, Teddy? Did you bury it?

Teddy growls.

Hey. It's me, Jacob McKnight. Wook what I've got. The bologna flops from his hands.

Teddy stops growling. Licks his chops.

Yes, thought you'd wike this.

Jacob takes another step. Teddy's ears relax, and his tail looks like it's thinking about a good wag.

There's a boy, there's a boy.

Jacob takes the last step. Puts his hand out.

Teddy snaps at the meat.

Nicely, says Jacob, take it nicely.

And Teddy takes the meat on his tongue like a Catholic.

That's a boy.

Teddy gobbles, wags.

Hungwee, weren't you? Poor guy. Always hungry.

Schloop, Teddy's tongue across Jacob's cheek.

Jacob laughs and wipes his face. Can't stay too long, he says, my dad might come home, and I have to take this glove to my friend.

Schloop.

Alvy.

Thump-thump goes the tail against the ground.

He knows tons about science and animals. And he lives in a house.

Schloop.

Can't live with me, goofer. No pets in apartments. Jacob goes to pet the top of Teddy's head.

And the teeth *g-knaksh* just miss his fingers.

Jacob somersaults backwards. You bugger! I *fed* you.

Teddy growls.

Yeah? You wanna be put down?

Crazy barking follows Jacob off the lawn. He looks at his fingers, over his shoulder. Teddy stops barking, walks round and round in circles so small he could be chasing his tail.

And over at the diamond the guys are already playing. Alvy's in the field. Has a glove on. Hey, Alv, I got you this one.

It's okay. Spielman's letting me use his.

And Jacob thinks *What?* Spielman never lets anyone use his glove.

Down by the backstop Cracker waves at Jacob. Hurry up, honky, you on our side!

Jacob jogs over. First two guys got out, Cracks says, but the Deaner's batting cleanup.

First pitch, Spielman nails it. Starts his home-run strut, but – Holy mutha! – Alvy dives like Daredevil and *whap* snags it.

Did you see that? says Jacob.

And Alvy chucks it in. Spielman stands there, hands on his hips. Little shit can hit, too, he says. Smacks hands with Alvy when Jacob's side takes the field. Says when the bell goes they should all sit together during assembly.

Sure have been a lot of assemblies this year. Year of the Child stuff. Nobody really cares except it's better than class and You never know, says Spielman, Shits Himself could blow anytime.

Shits Himself? Alvy asks.

McCluskey, says Spielman. The principal. 'Swhat we call him.

It's a disease, says Jacob, and I made it up.

The disease?

His nickname. Spielman says it wrong.

I can say it anyhow I want.

It's Shits Him*self*.

Go away, McKnight.

The principal shits himself? says Alvy.

If he gets all worked up, says Jacob. Has to run to the toilet or he rips one like you wouldn't believe.

Reeks, too, says Cracker.

How do you know? says Spielman.

Bulldog Quinn told me. McCluskey blew a mutha when he gave him the strap.

Quinn lies, says Spielman.

Inside, Mr. Kazinski makes a megaphone with his hands like in gym class and yells at everyone *not* to go to homeroom. Hey, goofballs, did you hear me? Do not go to homeroom. Line up here according to class.

In all the hustle-bustle Jacob ends up two lines over, behind Gimpy-Gail and her friends. Gail says Hi, Jacob McKnight, and her friends scrunch their shoulders and cover their mouths *tee-hee*. Jacob nods hello, runs his fingers through his hair like Spielman does around the chicks, but it just falls in his eyes and he has to turn around because his penis is erecting. He should say something because he can feel Spielman and Alvy and Cracker looking over, but it's like Broca's Area of Speech in his brain broke and he can't even think up a sound. But then all the lines, shuffle shuffle, start moving and Jacob just looks at his shoes, shuffle shuffle, until the gym, where there's this huge big photo above the stage of starving children from somewhere awful, and a banner that says The Future Is Theirs, The Responsibility Is Ours. Shits Himself is up onstage, hands on his hips, looking at the students like God at botched creation.

Then, over all the hubbub, Spielman says Who's *that*? and points. Jacob looks. Behind Shits Himself, just next to the lectern, sit Father McMannis from the new Catholic school and – *Holy jumpin* – a woman who could be in *Playboy* except she has clothes. Cracker says Foxy lady, and gets shushed and stared at by Mrs. Steutzel, who makes sure they all sit apart except for Alvy who's right beside the Deaner. Having a laugh and all. Jacob pretends not to notice, plays with the ribbons – ultramarine – on the UNICEF button that browners from Grade Eight are handing out to everyone. Leans this way and that. Why do they always have to sit on the floor? Dad says hard cold surfaces draw out piles. Maybe McCluskey's ass, the inside of his ass, itches and hurts all the time. Enough to drive him batty. Enough to make you cut him some slack. McCluskey's face is like from Mount Rushmore, but in it you can see, Jacob thinks, what it's like standing in front of a bunch of kids and teachers who've seen you nearly crap yourself. Mortifying.

McCluskey raises his big arm way over his head, waits for all the talking to stop and clears his throat twice. Adjusts the mic. Welcome all, he says. This year, 1979, marks, as you know, the International Year of the Child. And many of you in your classes have already worked on projects related to this very special year.

Here in Glanisberg, there are plans, as you may know, to tear down the old schoolhouse and to replace it with a park that will commemorate the child.

Jacob has a look round as McCluskey goes on. Most everyone's paying attention except Spielman, he's pricking his thumb with his UNICEF button – and eyeing McCluskey like he's looking down a barrel. You can tell he's trying to make it happen with his mind – C'mon, he's thinking, *do* it, shit your fucking pants. Alvy, though, his eyes float around like he can see spirits in the air that nobody else can. He's not really listening, but if you asked him after assembly what Shits Himself said he could probably tell you word for word. His brain's like an ECG.

McCluskey doesn't blather on forever today though, says there are distinguished guests here whose special job it is to tell us all about the Year of the Child. A tip of the hat, please, to Miss Sophie Lindstrom.

The foxy lady foxy-walks to the mic.

Over the clapping, Spielman lets a whistle fly. Miss Richardson slashes him a look, but people laugh. Even Sophie. Then she tugs on her top, sweeps her hand across the audience and says The future is yours. The responsibility, she says, looking at McCluskey, the teachers, the responsibility is ours. Miss Richardson nods. Mrs. Steutzel and Mrs. Bunko don't.

Good thing Sophie's a looker because she goes on with a bunch of blather about how much her work with the Canadian Council for Awful Places woke her up and all. You, she says, are the lucky ones, the happy ones. Maybe compared to the starving children in the picture she keeps pointing at. They have flies crawling all over them and die by the boatload and can't even go to school. Lucky to live to the age of ten.

Everybody's starting to squirm and fidget on the hard gym floor but trying to look sorry for the plight of the children. Except Spielman. He's still poking his thumb. Little blob of blood on it.

Sophie's got her knickers in a knot now. Voice all quavery. Maybe because more and more people aren't paying any attention to her. Our obligation, she says, looking round at the teachers, is to ensure that today's children are equipped. Physically. Emotionally. Educationally. For today. For the future. *Thank* you.

Clap-clap and all that. But Jacob has his eyes on the Deaner, and for a second, for a second, feels real sorry for him. His mum and dad have the moolah, but for a guy who grows flowers Mr. Spielman can be a real bastard. Bashes Dean pretty bad sometimes. Buys him stuff to make up. But even though he's got a minibike and his own CB, Dean probably doesn't feel too lucky.

When the clapping dies down, McCluskey gets back up and introduces old Father McMannis. Back in his old stomping ground, the Father. Dad calls Immaculate Conception the lapsed-Catholic school. Used to be where all the Catholics came till they got a brand-new school, St. Mary's, across the river. Then Immaculate Conception became regular where even Presbyterians could go. And Dad said That's where you'll stay, boyo, there'll be no more of the papal bullshit. Haven't been to mass since. Which is too bad because Father McMannis seems kindly. Warm voice. Like Dylan Thomas except raspier. He dabs his baldy head and thanks the beautiful Miss Lindstrom for those alarming statistics, but You know, he says, and adjusts the mic, the spirits, the spirits of children are starving, too. And so I've a poem for you now. A poem about the blessed Virgin.

Kids giggle and teachers go *Shh*. Father pays no mind. Puts his specs on. Sips water. Reads. The words slip like soft warm sand through Jacob's fingers, but when Father's done the air in the gym says *Hush* like the end of the Dylan Thomas record *I sang in my chains like the sea*, then hush, and everything looks the same but feels like it means a lot more, like the air is pregnant. Dad says bollocks to papist superstition and half the priests are buggers. But this Father doesn't seem like that. To fidgeting whispering kids around him Jacob says *Shh* as Father goes on.

It's true, he says, looking over his specs at teachers, that a child is a cause for fretting, but a child is also a delight. Someone unique in the world. The *revelation* of a being. Not just a someday adult, an impersonal 'student,' a resource like gas or oil. The child is a person who needs a healthy nation, a healthy society that enriches his mind and soul. But most of all the child needs the constant affection, love and understanding of parents. Very early in life can a child can be stunted.

Groan like a weed, thinks Jacob.

But a child, says Father, will always see through his parents', his teachers' selfishness, insensitivity, hypocrisy. If parents want loving and trusting children then they themselves must be loving and trusting and wise.

Old Father's got a good head of steam now, gently pounds the podium as he says The *fam*-lee the *fam*-lee the *fam*-lee *must* be nurtured in this age of restlessness and mobility and of the mentality that values *things* more than people. The child needs all the care that the family and society can give, in order that he may be sheltered, protected, given freedom and opportunity for a fully human life. Let us pray.

Jacob bows his head but cracks his eyes and has a look round – at brand-new sneakers, designer jeans, leg warmers this colour and that colour, shiny braids – he has a look round and he thinks of Dad, of how he says Lovely piece of fish in the fridge, and it's one thin fillet of sole, and even though it's more than those kids in the photo eat in a week it's sad, sadder than the smell of the Sally Ann. And it's sad that Dad had to grow up poor in Scotland back when there weren't Years of the Child, when you were out of school by sixteen and got yourself a trade, boy, that's you on your knees in a three-by-three dugout a mile underground, shucking out coal with a spade. Fully human life, thinks Jacob, and imagines Dad snorting Yeah, right, fully human life, guess that's why I come to Canada, for the fully human life.

Amen, says Father, and Jacob blinks hard, hard, to keep bits and blank away. Sees spots. Hears clapping like it's through a wall. Gives his head a shake, and there, clear now, is the Shits Himself, back at the mic. Before we bring the assembly to a close, I would like to say a few more words, so moving were the words of our guests today. Our school is commemorating this most important year in many ways, including the planting of trees. To symbolize growth. Potential.

McCluskey isn't looking too comfortable, and Jacob wonders if his insides are on the boil because of all the Catholic stuff. But then he reads the direction of McCluskey's stare. Looks over his shoulder, at Alvy, and Spielman. Alvy's little body is quaking all over. And Spielman, Jesus, he's sticking the pin of that button right into his knee. Gritting his teeth against a laugh. Jacob looks back at McCluskey's glare and –

Holy jumpin.

For a second or two the gym feels like a tomb, or – *boom* – like a bombed church. Everybody – teachers, too – looks at McCluskey. But it wasn't McCluskey. It was Spielman. He *cranked* one! Just sits there with that button sprouting out his knee and his face bursting red. Bent over and laughing so hard no sound comes out. And Alvy beside him looking round like it's nobody's bother. It's *totally* quiet.

Then Bobby Hollingsworth laughs and has to use his puffer and Jacob just can't hold it in anymore, he laughs so hard it echoes and then everyone starts. Even Mr. Kazinski, 'cept his moustache hides his mouth, and because Miss Richardson is glaring at Spielman, Mr. K makes like a tough teacher and marches toward the Deaner, hefts him under the armpits. That's when Alvy puts a hand on Mr. Kazinski's forearm and says It wasn't him.

Eh?

It wasn't him, sir. It was me.

Jacob stops laughing dead. His face, slack.

Spielman looks at Alvy, over at Jacob.

Really, says Alvy, it was me.

Then both of you, says Mr. Kazinski, will be coming with me.

All right, says Alvy, standing like it's no bother.

Spielman hangs his head when he and Kazinski and Alvy move around people, but when he comes by Jacob he looks over and mouths It was *me*.

And the Shits Himself, poor McCluskey, just clears his throat and concludes assembly like nothing happened, nothing at all.

After school Miss Richardson sends Jacob to the office, says Not to worry, he just wants to speak with you.

It's lying on the desk when Jacob walks in. He pretends not to see it.

McCluskey clasps his hands behind it when he sits down and tells Jacob that his cohorts got off lucky with a week's detention.

Cohorts? What does that mean?

You know what it means. You were part of that disgrace this afternoon.

I wasn't, sir. I swear. I was really listening to that assembly.

McCluskey sighs like a gust on a lake. I know what my nickname is, Jacob, and I know who made it up, and, regardless. Your laughter. Your disrespect. Was hardly. The appropriate reaction, this afternoon.

Jacob doesn't move.

Do you hear me?

Jacob doesn't move.

McCluskey sighs again, says If you won't listen to me you'll listen to this one day. He picks it up, and it lolls like a tongue.

I'm sorry, Mr. McCluskey.

You're sorry a lot, aren't you, Jacob?

McCluskey swivels in his chair and parts the blinds. Watches kids getting on buses. That was a, a, disgusting, disrespectful demonstration today, Jacob. Disgusting.

Jacob wonders what he's supposed to say, why they always say things that don't let you say anything while they wait for you to say something.

Quite, says McCluskey, the demonstration.

Jacob says Sorry, but it sounds like *all I did was laugh.*

Tell me, Jacob.

Sir?

This friend of yours. This Chatwin.

Alvy.

Yes. What can you tell me about him?

He's a good guy, sir.

A good guy. Consorting with the likes of Spielman. Why would a good guy pull – McCluskey spits his words – such a child-ish, inconsiderate stunt.

It wasn't, Jacob starts to say, but swallows his words – It wasn't Alvy – when McCluskey raises an eyebrow. When he imagines Spielman coming for him – You squeal on me, asshole? I dunno, Jacob says, I don't think ... Alvy meant to –

Exactly *his* explanation.

Jacob's eyebrows bend like cats.

Jacob, says McCluskey, I can phone Chatwin's mother. I probably will. I can ask for a doctor's note. Maybe I will. But – McCluskey glances at the strap – I want you. To tell me. Confidentially. If this Alvy Chatwin – he blushes, looks at the picture of the Queen – has ever complained to you. About a condition.

Jacob's eyebrows say *Sir?*

You know what I'm talking about, Mr. McKnight.

Jacob fights to keep his face straight when he sees it: Alvy, saving Spielman's ass by looking McCluskey straight in the eye and saying he has the shits. Can't help it, sir, it just happens. Ho-lee jumpin. His heart whams away but Jacob stops zygomaticus major from activating. Steeples his fingers all serious like a TV doctor saying If you want my *medical* opinion ...

Mr. McCluskey's eyebrows say *Well?*

Well, sir, please don't tell Alvy I said –

McCluskey opens his hand, nods and says Confidential.

We were down at the Riverbend Restaurant this one time, Alvy and me, and we had some pretty greasy fries, and Alvy, you could tell by his face he shouldn't have had any, and *please* don't say anything, Mr. McCluskey, but. He had to run. To the bathroom. You could hear it.

Hear what?

It was like a blowhole, sir. On a whale.

McCluskey rubs his big hand over his face. That'll do, Jacob.

Special underwear, sir. I think.

That'll do, Jacob.

Thank you, sir.

We're not done yet. I want you to know something. You seem to like this Alvy, and for whatever reason you continue to associate with boys like Spielman.

Dean can be okay, sir.

Uh-huh. Well. I would like you to think, Jacob, about other people, all people, like you think about your friends.

Jacob just looks McCluskey in the eyes.

Son, we all know you've ... been through a lot. This Chatwin, too. Losing a father so young.

Jacob's heart says *What?*

But there's still no excuse, McCluskey says, to be so selfish. To ... McCluskey swivels his chair. Pauses. Swivels back. His face is pretty hard to look at. Not angry. Just embarrassed and sad. Just *think* about other people, Jacob, that's all I'm asking. Learn to keep some things to yourself. The school, me, all of us, were dishonoured today. A joke. We were a goddamned joke. Jacob jumps when *bam* McCluskey slaps the desk. Starts standing. Teeth. Claws, his hands. But he stops. Sits. Starts blathering. Jacob isn't listening. Just keeps thinking Alvy's dad, dead. And Alvy never saying anything.

Do you hear me, Mr. McKnight?

Loud and clear, sir. I am sorry. Really I am.

Don't let me see you in here again.

No, sir.

Or there'll be nothing to laugh about. Nothing at all.

Outside the office, Jacob rips the UNICEF button from his shirt, hucks it down the hallway. Fingers the tear. Great. Dad sees that and it's a bang on the ear, Get out the needle and thread, boy. And a bang on the other ear if Jacob doesn't sew it perfect.

Screw you, McCluskey, says Jacob over his shoulder.

But it's hard to stay mad. Alvy's dad. Dead. And Alvy never saying anything. But you, Jacob thinks, never told him anything either. Like secret identities. Buried. Not everybody has to know everything. Maybe that's what Alvy thinks, too.

Jacob stops by the UNICEF button, but the caretaker pushing his big dust mop around the corner doesn't even blink. Behind him Jacob hears the button scraping along the floor. Like a bike beneath a car. He takes off, hard. Halfway to the hospital he remembers the rip in his shirt. Mends it back at home best he can.

Wonders when he pricks himself how the Deaner did it over and over until there was blood. Everyone's got secret identities. Things you should never know.

The Big Stink, that's what Jacob calls it, dies down in a week or so, but Alvy's not the New Kid anymore. He's kind of a hero. The Kid Who Blew the Big One. Plus, it's true, the little guy can hit – turns out he played Little League in Alberta – so he's in there with Cracks and the Deaner pretty good. They even say he should come to the factory on Sunday, see the Murph.

Who's the Murph? Alvy wants to know.

He is wawn crazy honky, says the Cracks, but he gives you free choc-o-let!

Only if you get in, says Jacob.

Oh, we're gettin in, says Spielman.

Sunday morning Dad and Jacob are out the door by eight. Stick in a solid six. Dad edges by in the last ten yards, says What was that, boy?

Hands on his knees – what is it this time? – Jacob spits and says Sorry.

Sorry what for?

Jacob looks up. Dad's got a grin on, says Fucken great, lad, you're startin to move. He whaps Jacob on the shoulder. Makes breakfast. Soft-boiled eggs, tea and toast, the whole lot. Jacob gobbles it all down. Thanks, Dad!

Where you off to in such a rush?

Just biking round. With the guys.

Careful.

Yup.

Spielman ripped off two *Hustlers* from his dad. They all have a look out back the factory. Jacob says Those are labia majoras and that is the clitoris. Dean licks it. Bobby has to have a haul. Two pumps. Cracker says Just one, remember? But Bobby can't talk. Just takes big breaths.

What's a matter, says Dean, never seen a cunt before?

Like you have, says Alvy.

Melissa Fowler's, says Spielman. I ate her out.

You lie, says Alvy all jokey-like but Spielman, Jesus, here he goes. I *what?* he says, and stands right close to Alvy, looks down at him.

C'mown, brothas, says the Cracks, we here for the choc-o-let!

Spielman stares for a second longer, and Alvy, holy shit, he stares right back, and the Deaner makes a fist but turns and hammers the door.

And everyone stays quiet. Jacob's heart, *wub*-dub, *wub*-dub.

Click-clack goes the lock, and, holy crap, there he is.

Well well, lookee here. The peckerheads.

Spielman looks at Cracker like he's an idiot when he says Asalamalakim. Looks back at the Murph. Gonna let us in?

Thought you forgot all about me.

Didn't forget.

Thought you didn't like me anymore.

Brought you something.

Brought me somethin?

Spielman holds up the *Hustlers* one in each hand like it's no bother, but he's shaking a little.

Ohh, says the Murph, dirty boys. Buncha dirty boys.

Want 'em or not?

Cracker takes a step back when the Murph leans out the door – and sees Alvy. Who the fuck are you?

Alvy blinks and says I'm Steve Austin, Six Million Dollar Man.

Smartmouth is what you are.

Alvy shrugs.

Four-eyed little smartmouth, says the Murph, but then he smiles. Ruffles Alvy's hair. Looks this way, that way. Scoops the *Hustlers* and says Okay, my boys. Holds the door open wide.

Holy jumpin. They're *in*.

And, *thoom*, the door closes behind them. Cracks, Alvy, even Spielman look smaller. Younger. Scared.

This way, boys.

Long and slow the Murph walks down the wide hallway. Folds the *Hustler*s in half, shoves them behind his belt. And whistles. Then he takes a jangly bunch of keys out of his pocket. Lets them dangle from the long long chain attached to his belt. Swings them *sa-woosh* in big slow circles. You comin, slowpokes?

Spielman leads. The Murph smiles. Keeps, *sa-woosh*, walking. Turns left down another long hallway. By the big doors at the end he picks a key. Thumbs it. I have all the keys, boys. My kingdom. Then he opens the big doors wide and Bobby says Holy cow.

Gleaming vats. Pipes – there must be miles – and they twist and turn like stiff intestines. Consoles with loads of buttons. Lights, blinking. And this noise, *mmm-ta-kash, mmm-ta-kash*, like the room's alive but having a snooze. Bobby wants to know why there aren't any people, and Cracker says It's Sunday, goof.

Blessed day it is, says the Murph. Day of rest. Except for the likes of me. But if ol' Shit 'n' Shinola upstairs – the Murph jerks his thumb – has his way, then there'll be people here Sundays, too, little porker. He ruffles Bobby's hair. Yep, round the fucken clock and every day of the goddamned year 'cept Christmas, and knowing him he'll have workers here on Christmas, too. Either way that's the end of my job and a fine family business thanks to Cocoa Puff up there.

And just when Jacob's about to ask if they can see the boss's office, Alvy wants to know how the chocolate gets made. Bobby, too. Spielman says Who cares, but the Murph says They care, and starts in. Raw cocoa goes in that big motherfucker there ...

Sounds to Jacob like the Murph's doing his best but also talking a lot of blather, so he follows Cracks and Spielman *clang bong* down steel stairs to where they have a good laugh staring at themselves all short and fat in the vats. But then the Murph puts his thumb and finger in his mouth and whistles, echoes everywhere. C'mon back up here, peckerheads.

Back in the main hallway, Jacob says Can't we go up to the top?

Sa-woosh.

What's up there? says Dean.

Director's office, says Jacob.

So what?

Sa-woosh.

So I wanna see it, says Jacob.

Me, too, says Alvy.

The Murph swings his keys like a pendulum. Wanna see the big man's office, do youse?

Jacob nods.

What about my office? I got an office. 'Bout the size of the big man's shitter. Why don't you come see my office?

Out the corner of his mouth Cracker says Let's get our lily asses out of here. Jacob's just about to give Cracker the nod, but the Murph says Just joking. Don't wanna see my office. Wanna see the big man's. Fancy pantsy. He wouldn't mind parting with some chocolate. Wouldn't notice a thing. Not for boys like you. The Murph looks at Alvy. Not for smart boys like you, he says, go on and be a big man yourself one day. Make the big money.

Maybe, says Alvy.

Maybe?

I will, says Spielman.

Oh, we all know you will, Petunia. Yeah, why don't you come upstairs with your tag-alongs, and we'll sit you down right in the big chair, you can see how it feels. Give some orders. Then we'll all ... we'll all have ourselves some treats. The Murph turns, starts walking *sa-woosh.*

I ain't going up there, says Bobby.

I am, says Alvy, and off he goes.

Spielman follows him.

And Cracker follows him.

Jacob tells Bobby he can wait right here if he likes, and he jogs away.

Bobby takes a haul on his puffer, follows.

The Murph stops by the elevator. Picks a key, puts it in the hole between Up and Down. Waits. I hold the keys, he says.

All the keys to the kingdom, says Jacob, and the Murph says Bingo, cranks his wrist *bing*, the doors slide open. In they go. You can smell the Murph's breath in here. Rum.

Bing.

Down a long hallway but it's got cushy carpet, burgundy, smells new. Left turn, so quiet up here, past doors – Operations, Maintenance, Marketing – all the way to the end. Right turn down another hallway, short, with old posters from a long time ago – Cook's Finest, From Our Family to Yours! – in frames, and all these awards with big gold seals like suns in the corners. At the end of the hall are big black double doors that say DIRE|CTOR. Here's where Shithead runs the whole show, fellas. Guess how much the little wog makes.

I bet at least twenty-five thou, says Jacob.

Spielman snorts, and the Murph nods. Try again, he says.

Thirty thou, says Jacob.

Maybe three times that.

Really?

Bet your little ass on it, kid.

Maybe he's really educated, says Alvy, maybe he works really hard.

Probly never had to work for a dollar in his goddamn life. Spoiled fucker. The Murph makes a fist and *whump* hammers the door. A *Hustler* falls from his pocket and flops open when it hits the floor. But nobody looks at it, just at each other. When the Murph bends down to get it, Spielman jabs his finger behind them and the Cracks nods.

Where youse goin?

Nobody says anything.

Sure you don't wanna come in? Nice in there.

Maybe next Sunday, says Jacob, and even though the Cracker's face says Are you nuts? Jacob looks over his shoulder. Pictures that office. A big leather chair like Neily Waldengarden's law office. Intercoms – *Please show him in.* Gold pens.

Sure, says the Murph. Next Sunday. If you're good enough. Good boys who do what they're told.

The elevator ride feels like forever. But back downstairs the Murph's all smiley. Talks normal. C'mon in here, he says, and get your treats. Takes them into a cafeteria. Lifts the lids of two big green bins. All yours, boys.

Heaps of it. Chocolate almonds and bits of bars all jumbled together.

But nobody moves. The Murph sits down, clomps his boots up on the table. Pulls out the *Hustler*s. Go on, he says, it's free.

Much as we want? says Bobby.

All youse can eat.

But nobody takes that much. Only what they can hold in two hands. Then they just stand there. Look at each other while the Murph flips pages and grunts. Then he holds up a woman. Chinese except with blond hair. Long red nails pinning her labia back like dissection. Like that, boys?

Spielman says Sure.

What about you, Blondie Four Eyes?

Alvy shrugs.

The Murph stares. Breathes. Puts his feet down.

Jacob gets ready to run.

Well. Guess youse gotta go. Leave the old Murph here all alone. All right.

The room lets out a big breath. But the hallway, *sa-woosh*, still feels very, very big.

What's your hurry, boys?

They walk a little faster. Maybe twenty feet to go. Bobby doesn't look too good.

Nobody's gonna give me a little kiss?

They're at the door. *Whap* goes the Murph's hand against it. He leans, and bends, and puckers.

Cracks looks at Spielman, Spielman looks at Cracks. Nods at the door and *boom* they bodycheck it.

They're out. And gunning it. Chocolate almonds falling everywhere.

Dean turns it on up Dead Man's Hill. Jacob passes Alvy. Passes Cracks. Eyes Spielman. Gains on him, but the Deaner starts laughing. Jacob, too. Then Alvy yells Stop. *Stop.*

And Jacob looks back.

Stops dead.

Alvy's pointing down the hill. At Bobby. Bent, gulping air.

Here comes Cracks and Jacob says Your brother, but Cracks blasts right by. Jacob screams his real name.

And Graham stops, looks.

Bobby, says Jacob, he can't breathe.

Cracker runs back. And Alvy. And Jacob. Checks his shoulder. Sees Spielman checking his shoulder, but still gunning it. Up.

Cracker *whap-whap-whaps* Bobby's back. Your puffer, where's your puffer?

But Bobby's just trying to breathe and Oh no, says Alvy, and points. At the puffer. On the ground. Back by the door. And the Murph, standing there. Watching.

Jacob looks at Cracks. Cracks looks at Jacob.

You're faster.

He's your brother.

Look at his eyes, says Alvy.

I'll get it, says Jacob, and he goes.

Has a look.

Goes.

Has a look.

But the Murph doesn't move a muscle. Just watches. And his face, it's not crazy. Not mad. More like Teddy's when he's stuck out in the rain. But Jacob keeps a bead on the Murph, bends, keeps a bead on him. And he's got it. Boom, gone. Checks his shoulder.

Just the door, closing.

Jacob, his heart whumping, makes Bobby stand up straight, puts the puffer to his mouth, and pumps. In, Bobby. Pumps again. Breathe it in.

Sounds like Darth Vader smoking, says Alvy.

Shudup, says Cracks.

Sorry.

You okay, little sucka?

Bobby nods, breathes Th-hanks, Jacob.

And Jacob says No sweat. But he's soaked. And shaking.

Up top of Dead Man's, Spielman's just standing there eating a chocolate bar. Watching them all. Having a laugh.

Bobby can't help it, cries. Cracks even holds his hand, and says You wanna go home? But Bobby shakes his head and knucklerubs his eyes. Makes himself laugh, and says I almost shit my pants.

On the way up Dead Man's, Alvy asks him if he ever turns blue, but that's all Jacob hears. The scraping sounds are in his head. And Mrs. Simpson bawling. And people coming out their houses. Just standing there and watching. Like Spielman. Face against the window of his old man's truck, staring when the policeman waved them through the intersection – and Jacob was running, the other way.

Up top Jacob just watches them at one another, it's all who was scared the most no way I'm goin back there that guy's a pervert you dropped your chocolate too bad. Spielman takes a big chomp and chews *Mmm* and rubs his stomach at everyone. Alvy shakes his head and says You were the chicken, Spielman.

Frig, thinks Jacob, here we go again. Hardman Dean. He walks up to Alvy, but stops. Like suddenly he remembers. The office. And Alvy, saving his ass. Here, crybabies, he says. Gives everyone some of his chocolate. And a little more to Bobby. They all sit down in the long grass. Don't say anything. Just eat. Turn their faces to the sun. But Alvs better watch his step. No one teases the Deaner, not even guys in Grade Eight, not even if you're on his good side. Three months after the accident when Jacob first went back to school it was like he had a force field or a disease. Everybody steered clear. Not Spielman. Like in gym when no one would wrestle Jacob or go too hard but Spielman took him down no bother, had the half nelson on him so hard Mr. Kazinski said Easy, goofball, Jesus. It's Field Day soon and right now Jacob wants to beat Dean Spielman. In the mile. Wants to beat him bad. He looks back down the hill, remembers that he was gaining. Then he looks at the door, where the Murph stood, watching.

Hey, Jacob, says Alvy.

Yeah?

See those birds?

What birds.

There, see? They're finches. *Carpodacus mexicanus.*

Wish I had my gun, says Spielman, and he gnaws his chocolate like a bone.

Not even two o'clock, but everyone goes home and not just 'cause of Spielman. More like, without saying anything, they all know they did something a different kind of scary. Not chucking rocks at cars scary, parents getting phoned scary. It'd be cops getting phoned if parents found out. Plus a shitkicking from Dad. So before he comes home from the hospital Jacob doesn't read comics. Scours the bathroom. And does two pages of anatomy. The bones of the skull. All the bits are done now, the bits Jacob could see. But all inside he was broken, too. Internal bleeding. Where do you start with internal bleeding? The spleen? The heart? Do you have to stop the whole heart? One of the bones of the skull is called temporal, which also means time. If you break your skull it can heal good as new in four to six weeks, but the heart never fully recovers even if you have an enlarged myocardial muscle from running.

Jacob flips pages, looks for where he can stop internal bleeding.

Stops when he sees it.

Stares at how different it is from the ones in *Hustler*. Those ones look furious. This one is quiet, but scarier, dead-looking. Jacob knows all the names of all its bits, but he hasn't coloured it yet, the cunt. In anatomy it isn't a cunt, it's a vagina, except if you're Bobby then it's the capital of Saskatchewan. *Va*, Jacob tells him, *Vvvv*, but Bobby has his own way of talking. Basghetti. Ambleeance. Mons *vvven*-eris, says Jacob out loud. And he picks purple. Gail McBride likes purple. So did Mum 'cept Jacob can't think of Mum and colour the vulva even though that's where he came from. Where they both came from except Jacob was second. Hard on Cailan's heels, said Mum, like you couldn't wait your turn. The wee bonus. That's what Dad said. Cailan was first past the post, but you were the wee bonus. Dad had his pecker in Mum's D2, Vaginal Orifice. The pecker is two pages back and it isn't one thing like it looks from the outside, it's lots of bits together like D, Corpus Cavernosum, and G, Superficial Fascia, which when Jacob reads it gives him a laugh. The Structural View of the penis makes it look like a rocket. It has many layers. Jacob and Dad have long prepuces. Spielman's always saying McKnight's dick has a turtle-neck. And his seminal vesicles are working, Dean says he gets sperm every time he pulls the goalie. Jacob doesn't. Dad ejaculated his sperm into Mum in Scotland. At the mine. It probably happened on a bed but Jacob pictures them way underground. Dark. In a deep secret place under Mount Cruachan where Dad worked Mine Rescue and Mum was the nurse. Should have seen your father, boys, he was a looker. When they were real little Mum always said that and smiled big and her teeth were white then.

Jacob closes *The Anatomy Coloring Book*. His bum's sore, but he keeps sitting there on the floor by his bed. Can hear the clock in the kitchen, *tak, tak*, but that's all. After a while he opens his sketchbook. Uses the purple pencil.

Dear Mum,

How are you? I am very fine. Dad and I are running every day, and he says I'm doon grreat, ha-ha. How is Alberta? I made a new friend, his name his Alvy and he lived in Red Deer.

Jacob stops. Crosses it all out. It's never what's in your head. What was it like in Scotland? He'd like to ask her that. When you and Dad were at the mine. What was it like when we were fetuses? When we were just little eggs? But things like that look crazy when you write them, and adults mostly don't like questions. Like it's a big pain to answer them, or they hardly tell you anything, or just can't. Like Dad. And Jacob hides the sketchbook 'cause he didn't even hear him come in and holy crap it's after five. *Whump* on the door. You in there?

Yeah.

Am I to cook as well after working all bloody Sunday?

Coming, Dad.

Through the bathroom door Jacob asks him if spaghetti's okay.

Not much sauce left, says Dad over the tap.

I'll water it down.

Jacob plops in a little ketchup – Dad never eats it anyway – to thicken it back up a little. Tastes not bad, but it's hard to swallow 'cause Jacob feels like he's got a throatful of questions that he can't bring up. See you, pay no mind to all that. That's what Dad'd say. Then go to his room.

Crazy dreams keep him up that night. Bits of the Murph – his teeth, the keys – all mixed up with Teddy thrashing at the end of his chain and growling at Dad who's barely far enough away and trying, *one* and *two, breathe, boy*, except it's Bobby and he's dying. Then Mum tells Dad everything's okay, but she looks more like Mrs. Chatwin.

Just two miles Monday morning, but what a slog – Jacob's tired from the dreams, plus it pours. Morning recess inside. Jacob and Alvy invent two new characters, Arsenal and X-Calibre. They both survived the nuclear holocaust, and they protect the City of the Living from mutant looters and Russians. X-Calibre regenerates like Wolverine except faster. Plus he is a scientific genius. He invented his gun which shoots plasma blasts and grappling hooks plus normal ammo, and he also designed Arsenal's armour. Arsenal almost died in the war and now he has to wear the armour forever because it pacemakes his heart. Arsenal is almost invincible – he can fly, he can stop rockets and lift cars – but every inch of him is covered and even if the radiation and Russians disappeared he'd still be imprisoned in the armour forever. So he is full of wrath, like Wolverine, and doesn't always act like a hero. Blasts Russians like crazy.

Then Spielman comes over and asks what they're doing.

Drawing, says Alvy, what's it look like?

Spielman looks over Jacob's shoulder, says Comics are dumb.

And Jacob just like that gets an idea for a supervillain. His name is Plague. The radiation warped his brain and his breath is like poison. When Spielman goes he tells Alvy.

Alvy says I like the Murph's name for him better.

Petunia?

Yeah! Alvy draws a goofy Dean face in the middle of a flower, and they have a good laugh.

Come noon hour there's still a puddle between second and third but the sun's blazing and Cracker – She be tails, sucka – calls the toss. Hesitates. But picks Alvy first. Who else are you gonna pick? Spielman's the other captain. His first pick should be Bulldog Quinn or Danny St. Jacques – good stealer – but he says McKnight, you're on my side. So Cracks gets Danny St. Jacques, too, and his team starts creaming the Deaner's. Plus something doesn't feel right. Almost like when Jacob knew, just knew that the tire would – Get your head in the game, McKnight! – and he can't concentrate, strikes out on his first at bat, and keeps flubbing easy grounders. The Deaner is steaming, I fucken *hate* losing, fucken *hate* it.

One out now, and the Deaner's up, taking warm-up swings and looking out past centre field like he's going to tag one from here to the factory. But he's too worked up, swings at a shitty pitch and doesn't get all of it, doesn't get half of it. Slow grounder, dribbling like a bunt out to second.

And Alvy's on second.

He snags the ball on the run and fires it over to Bobby – throw it as hard as you want, Bobby'll catch it – except he drops it because Spielman screams BWAH and stomps on the base.

Bobby says No fair!

And Dean leans right in his face and says What?

Nothin.

Even though Jacob's on Spielman's side, he shakes his head when he steps up to bat and says to himself What a goon.

Spielman, hands on knees and still breathing hard, says Move me around, McKnight.

Jacob usually cuts the ball down the right-field foul line, but pictures nailing a good one that beans Spielman between the eyes. Out cold. Stop beaking off at everyone all the –

The first pitch blows right by.

Everybody on Jacob's team moans and everybody except Alvy on Cracker's team laughs. Spielman holds his head and screams Get in the fucken game!

Screw you, says Jacob under his breath, but his chest gets tight, his face hot.

Here comes the pitch.

Jacob swings so hard he spins himself around and Spielman says Are you fucking blind? That was a ball!

And Cracker grins like the Joker. Leans in like he just wants a better look at Jacob striking out.

Jacob gives his head a shake. Glues his eyes to the ball.

Here she comes.

Even though it's a little outside, Jacob thinks he can pull it to the opposite field, but he doesn't get all of it. Hard grounder but Cracker dives and – I am the greatest! – snags it. An easy force, and Jacob runs a little slower so Alvy can make the double and be a hero.

But even though he's out by a mile Spielman still slides.

And you don't need an anatomy colouring book to know that Alvy's knee – any knee – isn't supposed to bend that way.

But Alvy doesn't make a sound. Just falls. Then rolls. And rolls. Pound pound pounding the ground.

Jacob runs fast as he can. Stop Alvy stop, lie still lie still.

Alvy stops rolling, lies flat on his back, but thrashes his head from side to side and hisses between his teeth.

Where does it hurt, Alvy?

My asshole. Where do you think? My knee.

I know! Which one?

Just leeme alone.

Alvy.

Leeme alone!

Guys from the game and a few others mull around and have a look. Did you *see* that? I *heard* it, from over there.

Miss Richardson's on yard duty and her radar's pretty good usually, but she still hasn't noticed, keeps talking to Gimpy-Gail McBride and her girlfriends over by the swings.

Jacob looks at Bobby. Go get her, *now*.

Bobby runs off and Alvy tries to get up. Groans.

Stay down, Alvy. Don't move.

Alvy nods, closes his eyes.

Spielman has a stupid grin on his face like Alvy's faking it.

Jacob clamps his teeth together to stop them from chattering. Stands and pushes through bodies. Stops just short of Spielman. Nice one, Dean.

Nice what?

You really hurt him.

He was in the way.

Bullshit. You didn't have to slide.

What are you gonna do about it, cry? Dean steps forward, bumps Jacob's chest. The goon's face is beet red – he knows he shouldn't have done it, but he always has to be Tiger Williams or Dave Schultz. Jacob says Yeah, you're the big man, Deaner. Why don't you beat up Bobby next time?

A lot of kids around now, that feeling in the air that says *fight*.

On a force, says Spielman, pushing Jacob, you take – *push* – the man – *shove* – out! Less you're too chicken to slide, like you.

Screw you, superficial fascia.

Everyone goes quiet, and Spielman screws up his face, says What did you call me?

You heard me.

Say it again. I dare you.

Why? Your brain wouldn't understand.

The crowd goes *Ooooo*.

And Spielman goes for Jacob.

Has him down, face in the grass and the headlock on when – *What* is going on here? – Miss Richardson breaks through the circle.

Quiet at first, then a few kids start telling Miss Richardson all at the same time what happened.

Spielman gives Jacob's neck a squeeze, says in his ear You're lucky, McKnight, before he lets him up.

Before Miss Richardson gets into the who started this and all that rubbish, Jacob points back at Alvy. His knee, Miss R, it's hurt bad.

But before Miss Richardson can get a word out Alvy drags himself to his feet, starts hopping off. Miss Richardson glares at Spielman, then says Al-vy?

I'm okay, says Alvy. Keeps hopping. Starts to cry, just can't help it, when he tries to put a little weight on his knee.

Miss Richardson looks at Jacob and Spielman and says I will deal with you two later.

It was just an accident, says Spielman.

Later, says Miss Richardson. And she jogs after Alvy.

Gimpy-Gail looks at Spielman like to say Accident, *right*, then at Jacob like she's saying You, a *fight*? Then she gimpy-jogs after Miss Richardson and says I'll help.

Jacob starts to follow when Spielman eyes everybody and says It was an accident.

Nobody says anything.

Spielman eyeballs Jacob, and between his teeth says You better not.

Not what?

Tell.

What, that you did it on purpose, even though he saved your ass?

Spielman stares.

What if I do tell? says Jacob.

I'll break every bone in your body.

Have to catch me first.

I will.

Last year in the mile Spielman lapped everyone. Everyone. Speedy Dean. Naturally fast. Never trains. And I'm gonna lap you again, McKnight, Mr. Big Runner. *Fartlek*, what the fuck is *fartlek*, diarrhea? It is, Jacob wants to explain, Swedish for *speed play*, which means you alternate your pace for aerobic and anaerobic benefits, but what's the point of telling Dean anything?

When Jacob tells Dad what Dean's been saying, Dad gets that look. Like Teddy before he snaps. Aye, well, we'll see what his fucken nibs has to say when he's watchin your heels.

I'm not sure I can beat him, Jacob says. Jacob's not sure anyone can beat Dean Spielman, except maybe Billy Mutton, from Brighton. Five feet nothing except he goes like stink.

You had better fuckingwell beat him, boy. All the distance you've put in.

Six miles and maybe I could beat Dean, Dad. But Field Day is just a mile, and he's so fast.

Don't worry. I'm no through with you yet.

And every day now, it's distance before school – plus intervals after. Running, running, running, while poor Alvy gimps around on crutches with a torn patellar ligament. It'll heal, but Jacob tells Alvy he's gonna beat Spielman good. Make him look like a dork.

First Dad and Jacob use the high school track but too many people watch. Spielman, too. Gives Jacob the heaves. So they go up to the old horsetrack where Dad started running with Neily Waldengarden. Couple of times Neily shows up in his flash new car, a Honda Prelude. Jacob, Jacob, you're looking great, big boy. Thanks, Neily! Pay no attention, boy, and mind your form. Head up. Pump the arms. *Breathe.*

Two slow laps to warm up, then – *Go* – Dad hits the stopwatch *bang* and Jacob turns it on. Eighty per cent, quarter of the track. *Stop.* Back to a trot for another quarter, then – *bang* – *Go*, boy, *that's* it.

On the way home, even with the car window down, horse smell stays in his nostrils, his sweats. One day a jockey, seems pretty fat for a jockey, clucks his tongue and reins his horse in a bit, draws alongside Jacob for a look.

Jacob's supposed to be trotting, but he picks it up.

The jockey has a laugh and says Think you're fast, kid?

Jacob takes off.

And way down the bottom end of the track Dad yells What are you doon, boy? Stop!

But Jacob guns it hard, hard, and he's ahead, *he's ahead of a horse*, and he's smiling, and the jockey's laughing, drawing alongside. Flicking his whippy stick.

Then he and the horse are gone.

And Jacob looks at the massive haunches, the skin glistening in the sun.

Rounds the bottom bend, slows, stops. Hands to knees. Spits. Like acid.

Dad's shadow between his feet. Jacob looks up.

Dad hands him the water bottle, says Drink.

Jacob guzzles. Pours it on his face and hair. And *bang*, gets one on the ear.

Don't be a fucken showboat.

Sorry.

Dad points and says Car.

On the way home Jacob's ear hums like telephone wires but he doesn't care. He felt it. Felt his heart, booming huge big like a horse's. He felt fast.

Are you gonna be nice to me today?

Teddy doesn't look sure.

I bwot you somesing ...

Teddy's eyes say *Really?*

And Jacob holds out the sausages. Two, he says. One for me, and one for you.

Thumpity.

Okay. I'm coming over there now, 'kay? Jacob takes slow, small steps.

Teddy takes slow, small steps. Puts his snout out. Sniffs.

And Jacob gets down on one knee. I'm not gonna pet you, he says. Just gonna feed you. Nice-ly, nicely take it, that's it, good boy. No, this one's mine. Here, lick my fingers.

Schloop-schlalp-schloop.

Tickles. I saw you last night. Out in the wain. I know, it's terrible.

Schloop on Jacob's mouth. He wipes it and laughs and says Was gonna show you to my friend, Alvy, I told you about. 'Cept he's too scared to come over on his crutches.

Teddy whines.

Jacob pats his head slowly, says You have to be nice to Alvy, too. Spielman buggered his knee.

Thumpity.

Mean Dean.

Teddy bark-barks.

Exactly, says Jacob. Then Teddy puts his snout between Jacob's jaw and shoulder. Whines and nudges.

I don't know if I can beat him, Jacob says. It's in two days, the race, and every time I think about it I wanna puke my guts out.

Teddy sneezes. Moves back. Sneezes.

Where's your water bowl, boy? Chuck not even giving you water anymore?

Teddy just stares.

Bampot, says Jacob. Doesn't he know you have to drink?

Teddy barks soft.

Don't drink you'll die.

Woof.

Hang on. Jacob has a look. Sees the tap and hose. Gets up slowly and goes to the side of Chuck's house, and Teddy barks 'cept not like he's mad. Like he thinks Jacob's going away. Jacob says Shh, silly, someone'll see and tell my dad.

Woof.

Shush, I said. He'd *kill* me.

Teddy's all quivery. Jacob keeps pulling on the hose till he finds the end, then cranks the tap. Comes back. Teddy jumps like a gazelle. Tries to bite the water. Don't eat it, says Jacob, drink it. Watch. Jacob takes a slurp. Holds the hose back out. Teddy gobbles water and shakes his head and sneezes and barks. Gobbles more and sneezes again. Jacob holds the hose higher and has a laugh when Teddy jumps and jumps and almost bites the water. Then Jacob puts his thumb over the end and *spssash* gives Teddy a spray. Drops the hose and runs back a bit when Teddy shakes himself. And runs after Jacob. Who flops on his back and lets Teddy lick his face all over.

Dad's on afternoons the day before Field Day and it's a rest day anyway, so Alvy gimps it all the way down to Becker's then the library with Jacob. Shows Jacob his drawings of X-Calibre. He's got one of those masks that cover everything except his hair, which is long and white like Storm's from the radiation, and you can't see his eyes, they're just white like on old statues of Greek guys. Plus his cape is wide as a wall and billowing way out behind him.

That's excellent, Alvy.

Thanks.

I haven't got any drawings of Arsenal yet.

Alvy shrugs. 'Sokay, he says, then *whap* he slams the toffee on the table.

Just running and school, running and school.

Yeah.

Your knee getting better?

I'm off crutches day after tomorrow.

Wish Spielman had the bum knee.

You can beat him. Bite?

Not supposed to.

How come?

My dad says. Just carbohydrates. Before the race.

Have this piece. It's little.

'Kay.

Alvy's cheek bulges way out when he wedges a big triangle in. He sucks spit down and says Oo dwaw Aw-sun-ull, I oh-ing to staw a stowy-boad. And he starts right in.

Jacob starts with vital organs. Lungs, liver, the heart, which he enlarges a little. Then encases the lot in bones. Completes the skeleton. Adds the first layer of muscles. That's when Alvy looks over and almost chokes on his toffee. What's *that*?

Arsenal, Jacob says.

You're drawing his insides?

Everything, says Jacob. Layer by layer.

How come?

Jacob shrugs. More real that way, he says.

So how big's his wang gonna be?

Jacob does a quick Sagittal View like in the colouring book but way bigger. *That* big, he says. Alvy has a laugh and draws eyes and a mouth in the glans like Picasso except he says It's Dean Spielman, the biggest dickhead on the planet Earth. Then they laugh so hard Mrs. Bailey gives 'em the heave. Old bag, says Alvy outside but like usual he goes quiet on the way up Bridge Street. Jacob looks around for any old thing to say and sees a man painting the public pool by the new park. Hey, he says, look.

Alvy looks.

The pool, says Jacob. That guy's painting it.

'Swhat makes the water blue.

You like swimming?

Not really. Used to take lessons. When I was a little. Had to stop. Alvy draws his finger along the scar on his jaw.

Oh.

Alvy's quiet for a bit, then he says My brother's good, though.

And Jacob stops dead. You've got a brother?

Yeah.

You never told me.

Alvy shrugs. They keep walking.

How old is he? says Jacob.

Twenty-one.

That's way older.

He's my half-brother. We had the same dad.

Oh. Jacob pretends he didn't hear *had*, even though Alvy's face says Jacob can ask if he wants. He doesn't. Just asks Alvy if he likes the new park. It has a big rock in the middle with a plaque that says Commemorated in 1979, The Year of the Child. But Alvy just shrugs and says Can you?

Can I what?

Swim.

Not since when I was really little, says Jacob, blinking at old bits – Dad tossing them *splash, splash* off the dock. Why are you thrashing about, boy? Look at your brother. Yeah, Jakey, look at me!

It's awful at the top of the hill. Awful. Like before a race, or a long run. Alvy's face all tight, and Jacob with a throatful of words, wanting to ask. If he can come to Alvy's place. Eat pork chops. Play Payday. Alvy might be embarrassed at first but then it'd be all right, his mum has violet insides and besides anything's better, anything, than going home by himself again. Watching anything that comes on telly to pretend he's not scared, lying in bed and listening to the clock in the kitchen – *tak, tak, tak* – till Dad comes home.

See you tomorrow, Jacob.

You're coming?

Yeah.

'Cause you don't have to. Jacob nods at Alvy's knee, says You could stay home and the teachers would let you. It's Field Day all day.

I want to come see.

Jacob swallows. You need me to help you get home?

No.

'Cause I could help you. No sweat.

Alvy looks up Booth Street like he's thinking about it, but says It's okay.

And Jacob says 'Kay, see ya, then jogs off like it's no bother. But at home after spaghetti and the dishes he gets down on his knees with his elbows on the bed and prays his guts out. Crawls under the covers. And curls like a C, fists up under his chin. All shaky when he breathes.

Son, says Dad through the bedroom door. But Jacob's been awake for ages. Imagining every second, every stride.

Let's go, up.

Coming, Dad.

Breakfast is a slice of dry toast, plus a banana and a glass of electrolytes. Jacob expects a talking to. Strategy, tactics. But Dad doesn't say anything. Just shaves and gets his uniform on. Stops at the door on his way out. Turns and points at it. See this, he says.

Jacob nods.

Don't come through it again without a One pinned to your jersey.

Jacob nods, swallows sick.

Everybody at school's hopped up like huskies before a sled race. All the teachers got there way early to finish getting everything ready. Even Mrs. Bunko and Mrs. Steutzel. They're setting up water stations and laying out the ribbons on big fold-out tables. Suppose you'll be winning one of these? says Mrs. Steutzel when Jacob walks by for a look. He just shrugs, feels between his fingers the purple Third Place one – it's prettier, he thinks, than First, blue, or Second, red.

Well, best of luck to you, says Mrs. Bunko.

Jacob nods thanks, walks way across the playground toward the track. Doesn't want to see anyone right now, not even Alvy. Not a soul.

Right after first bell everybody assembles on the tarmac and gabs until Shits Himself and Mr. Kazinski start yelling through megaphones. Boys in one group, girls in another, then line up according to age and event. Event number one – just like every year – is Boys, Senior, the Mile.

And Cracker says Oh god. He can run a mean eight-hundred, but the mile totally psyches him out. Not Spielman. Has his wolf grin on. You ready, McKnight?

Jacob shrugs.

Bet I can still beat you.

I dunno, Dean, says Cracks, he be wawn fast mutha now.

Yeah, you won't even run, Hollingsworth.

Watch me, jive-ass turkey. But Cracker doesn't look too sure. Cracker looks grey.

Here comes Mr. Kazinski, jogging over with his clipboard. Okay, kiddies?

Nods.

All right, he says, let's get at 'er. And he throws Jacob a wink.

The butterflies start on the walk to the track. Jacob has to jog ahead, knees up-up, up-up, and give his head a shake *phooh*. Lots of events don't start till after the mile's over, and there's a whole big crowd lining up two deep all the way round to watch. *Phooh.* Dad's voice in his ears: Stay tucked in, boy, keep your form. Cracker can't keep his. Holds his belly and his cheeks b-ba-balloon. Told you, says Spielman, who gets a look from Miss Richardson when she says Come with me, Graham, and leads Cracks to a water station. There's one down. Jacob checks out the others while he stretches. Pretty sure he can beat them. Except maybe Pete Jameson, he's pretty good. Danny St. Jacques – goes out fast, but usually fades. Still came in ahead of Jacob last year, though. And the Deaner, look at him. Just standing there, arms crossed, not even stretching. Mr. Kazinski clicks his bullhorn and says *One* minute.

People start cheering already. Some even for Jacob. He looks up. There's Alvy, crutches in his armpits, clapping, and Gimpy-Gail hopping on her good leg, and a couple of the Little Bastards from Bulldog's pack give Jacob a dude nod, too.

Jacob nods back, gives his calves an extra stretch. Feels bits coming and blinks hard, Not now, please, not now, and they stop when Mr. Kazinski clicks his bullhorn and says Rrunners, to the line!

Jacob zips right to the inside.

And Spielman nudges in right beside him. Elbow to elbow.

C'mon, Jacob!

Go, Dean!

Mr. K says Quiet please, takes a stopwatch and starter gun from a tote bag by the milk crate. Sets the watch. Steps up on the crate.

And Dean whispers You better go hard, McKnight – Jacob closes his eyes – 'cause I am gonna massacre you.

Rrunners, take your marks.

Jacob lowers his eyes. Bends his knees.

Rready. Mr. K raises the pistol.

Bang.

Spielman *fucker* elbows Jacob in the ribs straight away, and other guys pile over to the inside lane way before they're supposed to. In a real race they'd all be disqualified, and Jacob has to sprint almost full blast to get by them all and duck in back of Spielman.

But it's … easy. Holy jumpin. It's *easy.*

Jacob checks his shoulder. Danny St. Jacques is going hard but the rest are well back. By the second turn. And Spielman – Jacob holds his breath a sec, listens – Spielman's breathing *hard.*

Nice pace, Dean.

Phooh-*hah.*

How you feeling?

Phooh-*hah.*

Not too good?

Screw you, says Dean, but he can barely get it out.

Jacob stays tucked in right behind him. Trots along. Moves out. Tucks back in. Wishes Dad could see. That's it, boy, test your man. See what he's got and save it for the kick. But when they come round the bottom turn of lap two Melissa Fowler, Dean's slutty girlfriend, gives Jacob the finger and says C'mon, Dean, cream that fruit.

So on the way by Jacob flips her the bird and moves out front. Alvy holds up his crutch like X-Calibre's gun and says Go, Jacob!

And he does. He goes. Hard. Dad's voice in his head says Easy, now, easy, save it, but Jacob wants to lap them, all of them, like Spielman did last year.

He catches the stragglers. Laps them.

Eyeballs Pete Jameson. Laps him.

Eyeballs Danny St. Jacques.

Boy, you're goan too hard.

But it doesn't feel hard. It feels like nothing. Like his body's empty.

Except he remembers.

He remembers. Not just bits and pieces and bloody mess, but everything even from when they were little in the house by the river. He sees it. The house, the river, the birdfeeder, and Dad, tossing seed. Whistling and singing to them all when they came. And the time when he gouged his thumb with the chisel from fixing up the old flatbottom boat and Mum hummed when she wrapped his hand. He sees that and birthday cakes and Mum's fancy *pahties*. He sees the stop sign and the flowers all piled high on the coffin and the race down the hill like in a big picture right in front of his eyes with everyone on the other side yelling and screaming Look, *look*, Spielman's catching him.

Jacob breathes gaspy like he just woke up from nightmares. Has a look round. *Spielman*, Alvy yells, waving a crutch, and Mr. Kazinski's leaning into the lane and screaming *Kick*, Jacob, *kick*.

Jacob checks his shoulder. Jesus. He's there. Spielman. All teeth and spit and pumping arms. Coming for him.

Last turn.

Jacob forgets Dad's drills – Head up, boy, pump the arms, lift the legs – and runs like a dog's right on his heels.

Crowd's going nuts. Jacob bears down.

Checks his shoulder.

There's Spielman.

There's the line.

Jacob *leans* ...

And feels teeth in his tongue when he hits the ground and Mr. Kazinski yells He did it!

Jacob rolls, wants air, swallows blood. Rakes the grass. And then he's up in Mr. Kazinski's arms. Your time, Jacob, look at your time! Mr. Kazinski holds up his stopwatch. Jacob blinks. Looks again. His first sub-five mile. Mr. Kazinski slaps him on the shoulder and says You did it, Jacob, then steers him to the water table. Miss Richardson hands him a cupful and Jacob gulps and spits bloody water and says I did it, Miss R, I did it. Leans into Mr. Kazinski's armpit when Spielman walks by and says Hey, McKnight, tell your dad he did a good job.

Mr. Kazinski shoots Dean a look and tells him to be a good loser, too.

Here comes Shits Himself, nodding, mile-wide grin on his face. A tip of the hat, Jacob, a tip of the hat. We'll be cheering you on at Regionals?

Sure, sir.

Well done.

Thank you.

Spielman doesn't even bother with his ribbon, and Jacob doesn't bother with any other event, case he pulls something. Just hangs around with Alvy. And watches Dean take first in the hundred metres, the two hundred metres, the long jump and the high jump. Dean asks for the bar even higher than it has to be. Clears it no sweat.

Show-off, says Mr. Kazinski, but he can't help smiling. Dean is amazing to watch. Takes second in the eight-hundred, but says he let Cracker win. Mr. K looks at Jacob like to say Will you get a load of this turkey, but Jacob doesn't care. Still can't wait. Takes off after everything's over, stops outside Chuck's even though he's out on the stoop, drinking a beer. Teddy comes out his doghouse and Jacob says I did it, boy, I did it. Teddy barks and jumps even though Chuck says Shut up.

You shut up.

Chuck goes to get up, but Jacob takes off. Runs all the way to the hospital, hard as he can. Bangs on the door of the ambulance office. Jim Digby lets him in. Hey, kid, how's she goin?

Super. My dad here?

Doin a rig check. C'mon through. See you got a ribbon there.
First. In the mile.

Old man'll near shit. At the door of the garage Jim yells
Johnny!

Hallo!

Boy's here.

Eh? Dad pops his head out the back of 399.

Me, Dad.

He sees it. Hops out and leaves the doors open behind him.
Jacob tries not to look at the stretcher, the fracture board. Watches
Dad instead. He takes the ribbon between his thumb, the one with
the little scar, and his forefinger. Feels it. Now, Jim, what do you
think of that?

Bee's knees, Johnny.

First, says Dad. And what was your time, son?

Four fifty-eight, Dad.

You're fucken jokin ...

Nope. I did it, Dad. I broke five.

The friggin wind! Right, that's us down to Jimmy's Pizza!

Spaghetti parmesan?

Whatever, says Dad, you frigginwell want. And in the big
garage Jim Digby's big laugh booms.

G'wan home, says Dad, and get yourself showered and ready.

'Kay.

On the way, Jacob jogs by Spielman's, but he doesn't see Dean
or his dad, he sees the factory director's flash Jag pulling out of the
parking lot. Maybe the Big Man bought a bunch of flowers for his
wife or for a date, but you can't see in the car. It cruises up to the
stop sign. Turns right. Jacob follows it. Feels like he can catch
anything. Even the Jag. Goes hard after it down Oliver and it's like
the director must see him in the rearview because he's not going
fast, but just when Jacob's about to touch the trunk he guns it and
zoom the car is gone.

The idea hits him soon as he's through the door and sees it. The phone. But he has a shower first. Can't get it out of his head, though, and his heart is thudding faster than in the race.

After he's done getting ready there's still almost half an hour to wait until Dad gets home. Jacob sits on the edge of his bed. Listens, *tak, tak,* to the clock. Bites his lip. Goes to the phone. And dials zero.

Operator.

Hello. I need to call someone.

Is it an emergency?

No. It's my mum.

Where does your mother live?

In High River.

Ontario?

No. Alberta.

The operator gives Jacob the number for directory assistance. He calls it. McKnight, he says, Trudy McKnight, and just when the lady says she has no one by that name Jacob remembers and says Wilson, it's Wilson, and she gives him the number. He says it over and over on the way to his room. Writes it down in his sketchbook. Goes back to the phone. Stares at it, heart booming. And dials. Three rings, he tells himself, if no one answers after three rings –

A man's voice says Hello? Hello?

And Jacob says Sorry wrong number, like it's all one word before he slams down the phone. Sits there till he hears Dad thumping up the stairs.

Hey hey.

Hi.

Ready?

Jacob nods.

Right. Just let me get washed and we're out the door.

Jacob looks at the phone while Dad scrubs his face and neck. Feels sick to his stomach. But down at the restaurant Jimmy brings over a big chocolate milkshake without even asking, and Dad says Go on then.

Jacob takes small sips.

What's wrong?
Nothing.
Then enjoy it, frigsakes.
I am enjoying it.
It won't last. Believe me.

But even the next morning Dad has eggs and the whole lot on first thing. Breakfast first? says Jacob.

Rest day, son. Tomorrow, too, what the hell. Get back at it Monday.

The toast pops and Dad drums the countertop. Halves or soldiers? he says.

Soldiers, says Jacob. Better for dunking.

Right you are.

Dad piles the soldiers on a side plate. Doles out the eggs.

Right then, kid, get that in you now. We've somewhere to be.

We do?

Dad nods.

Where?

Surprise.

Jacob swallows soldiers almost whole.

And two hours later, walks out of Athlete's Foot in Peterborough wearing a pair of Villanovas. Brooks, says Dad, top o' the line.

Jacob puts weight on one heel and says Fit good, too.

Hope so. You'll be loggin the miles in them, let me tell you.

Miles is right. More miles, more intervals, more *fartlek*. And faster, faster. But he's not fast enough. It's your confidence, boy, what's happened? It's like you don't want it. You've got to want it.

If Jacob could tell Dad the truth, then he'd say he doesn't want it. That he *doesn't* even want to go in the damn stupid race. That it will be summer soon, and he just wants to draw comics with Alvy in the library after school, or go bird hunting with Cracks in the orchards. But even if Dad didn't bash him one he'd say Fine, suit your-fucken-self, boy, see if I care. And that would be worse. Somehow that would be worse. Even though Dad gets Jacob's

EMCA quizzes bang on, he's sitting up more nights than usual staring at the turned-off TV, and in bed Jacob hears the ice cubes tinkling, the night hisses – *You bloody bitch, you.* So one Saturday that's only supposed to be a slow two-miler but Dad says he's no feelin too well, Jacob goes out alone. And guns it. Let me win, my ass, Spielman. I'll show you and I'll show Billy Mutton, too.

But he can't settle in. Sky's like lead this morning, and wind makes the trees hiss. Gives him the shivers. He spits. Checks his shoulder.

Empty road.

At the one-mile marker he starts to turn. Stops and says No, fucksakes, I'm doin it. Keeps going and turns into the park. Jumps the gate chain. Turns left and goes hard. For the hills.

Leans in. Arms up. Lungs working now. Checks his shoulder, crests the hill.

And lets himself go.

Faster.

Closes his eyes against them. But no bits come. Just Mum's voice in his ears, *You did it*, but he lets the hill take him and halfway down he's flying, hears nothing but *whoosh*.

And attacks the next hill, too.

Turns at the top, jogs on the spot for a sec, then down he goes again. Then up, last one, and – C'mon, he says, c'mon – down. And the momentum takes him all the way back to the gate. Hands on knees. Spits. And looks back at them.

Did it, he says.

Then looks up. Thunder. And fat raindrops, *pap ... pap-pap*, like the sky's got a bloody nose. Jacob takes off, hopes he won't get a soaking. Jumps – *Jesus* – when lightning splits the sky like a skull and down it comes in sheets. He picks it up but can't stop shivering. Knows it's just wind in the trees but swears he hears it. His name. He looks back, blinks the rain from his eyes. And swears he sees him, dragging his massacred ankle and trying to say *Stop* with his saggy busted mouth. Blinks again and it's Spielman, *You better fucken run.*

Mind your form, he tells himself. Breathe.

Every stride a splash and the soaking singlet hanging off him. Dad'll be steaming. Why in fuck were you out in that, boy?

When Jacob hears the car horn he gets way over on the shoulder. Looks. Looks again and holy fuck it's the Murph, cruising right alongside him, grinning out his open window. Big dog in the back, one of those black and tan bastards with the slobbery mouths. Barking. Trying to get in the front. The Murph smacks it and says Get back there, then grins again.

Hey there, Long Legs.

Jacob looks straight ahead. Tries to keep his breathing right.

You're all wet.

Jacob goes faster.

Need a ride?

No.

I can give you a ride. He doesn't bite.

My dad's coming to get me!

But the Murph keeps cruising right along beside him. Checks the road ahead, behind, says Haven't seen you in a while.

Jacob goes faster. The Murph keeps up. Or your friend, he says, your little white-haired friend.

Phooh, ha, *phooh*, ha.

Should come by and see me again sometime.

Get out of here! Jacob takes off, full sprint. Looks back, but the Murph's just turning into his laneway.

Back at home, Jacob sneaks up the stairs, ducks in holding his shoes and socks. But Dad's right there at the table, studying.

Jesus Christ, look at the state of you.

I went a little farther, says Jacob, but he can't help his teeth chattering.

A little? says Dad, and he nods at the clock.

I did hills, Dad. Went at them hard.

Up Dad gets and Jacob gets ready for it, *bang*, but watches while Dad goes to the washroom and comes out with a towel. Get those off, he says.

Jacob strips, and Dad scrubs him till he's red and raw. There now, go on. Get yourself showered.

'Kay.

And see you.

Yeah?

I'll tell you when to do hills, hear me?

Jacob nods, nods.

What are you crying for?

Just I got scared.

You'll live. Now go on and get showered. I'll make tea.

Lunch hour next day, Jacob cuts his speed work short. Gets his sketchbook and pencils and heads behind the portable. Stops when he sees Bulldog and the Little Bastards smoking Peter Jacksons. One of the bastards says Fuck off, but Bulldog says It's all right, McKnight's cool. Steps on his butt and comes up to Jacob. Spits in the dirt and says Fucken regionals, eh?

Yeah.

Soon, ain't they?

Few days.

Put 'er right fucken there, man, says Bulldog, and he gives Jacob a dude handshake, tells the Little Bastards This guy is fast, and he's gonna win that motherfucker.

Yeah man.

Fucken eh.

Beat those Brighton fags.

Then another Bastard does the *Rocky* song, and Jacob makes like he's laughing.

Bulldog gives his bangs a toss and leads the Little Bastards off. Looks back and pumps his fist *yeah man* and Jacob pumps his fist *right on* and thinks what a bunch of bampots. Watches them sneak up behind Gimpy-Gail at the swings and yank her bra strap. Gail tries to chase them. Sees Jacob watching. Stops and waves. Jacob's heart goes *wallop* and he ducks around the corner all hot in the face and has fantasies like in *Hustler* but with comics – he's flying way over the school and swoops down, bashes all the Bastards and Gail lies down under the monkey bars and Jacob is seminal. It's embarrassing when you're nice to a girl but think at the exact same time how you'd like to kiss her nipples, so Jacob flips to a new page, peeks round the portable once more to get a good look at Gail's gimpy leg. Starts drawing a tib and fib. Anterior and lateral views. Unbroken. Unbendy. Then he attaches the Achilles tendon and makes the gastrocnemius and soleus muscles like comic-book legs. Like Elektra. Black Widow. Wasp. Maybe one day Gail when she stops pubescence will be able to get the operation. Maybe Jacob will be the doctor. The surgery was bang on, Gail, your leg is stronger and better than before. O Jacob, kiss my Mound –

Big shadow on the page. Thought I'd find you here.

Jacob covers up, cranes his head. It's Mr. Kazinski. Big grin on and jelly doughnut dust in his moustache. Drawing again, eh, Picasso?

Jacob nods, tucks the pencil behind his ear.

Mind if I ask what?

Arsenal.

Mr. Kazinski shrugs.

Crippled superhero, cybernetic armour.

What about you, Road Runner? Do your wind sprints?

Yeah, where were you?

Sorry, couldn't make it. Teacher stuff. But I've got some good news.

Jacob's eyebrows jump. Brighton, he thinks, had a big fire, or Billy Mutton broke his leg. What's up, Mr. K?

I won't be putting you in the mile at Regionals.

Jacob's eyes bug out. But he wrinkles his face, tries to sound mad. Why's that, sir?

Just heard there's a three-thousand this year. Nobody tells me anything. Anyway, distance is your thing, Jacob. Takes you four laps just to get warmed up.

So?

So I put you in. Leadoff event, buddy boy.

I'm in the three-thousand?

You. And I'm pretty sure Billy Mutton isn't.

The bell rings. Jacob jumps up – See ya in gym, Mr. K! – and sprints across the playground.

But Dad's even quieter than normal over dinner. Did I cook it wrong?

Eh?

The spuds. Mashed enough?

They're fine.

I'll mix the bangers in next time, and fry up some on–

I've a bit of bad news, son.

Jacob stops chewing.

It's my EMCA exam.

Yeah?

Next week that's me down to Belleville. Two bloody days.

Am I staying with Neily?

It's not that I'm worried about. Second exam's on your race day.

Can you wait and write it some other day?

Son, I've only just finished paying for that fucking collarbone. Twice a year they exams happen. Sooner I get my EMCA, sooner I get on full-time. Benefits and all. Get your teeth looked at finally. Mine as well.

So you can't come?

I'm gonnae try. Second exam's just the mornin, like. What time's your race?

I think, Jacob lies, Mr. Kazinski said two.

Fucking hell ... It's old Doc Anderson who's doin the practical. Knows me. I'll see if I can duck out a wee bit early, make it down.

Brighton's pretty far from Belleville.

No kiddin.

Jacob scoops a forkful. Hope you can make it, Dad.

Whether I'm there or no, just win the hoor.

Next day at noon Jacob zips across the street, coast clear, and tells Teddy ... And I get to stay with Neily ... Cornelius Waldengarden ... He has a new Honda Prelude ... and a new dog, too ... Not as pwetty as you. That's wight. Have a pat on the head. *Ohhh*, belly, belly rubs yes, all you want is some lovin *hey*, easy, that's my hand –

Jacob hears – *bam bam* – a fist on glass.

And Teddy's up.

Jacob looks over at Chuck's place.

Bam bam bam.

Over his shoulder.

And Teddy shows his teeth.

Hey, it's okay, says Jacob, but he gets up, slow, backs off.

And, behind him, hears a window slamming open.

BOY!

It's Dad. Leaning way out his bedroom. What in *fuck* are you doing?

Teddy growls.

Get *away* from there! Now!

Jacob looks back at Teddy. It's okay, boy, he says, but he backs off, backs off, hears the apartment building's front door fling wide open and looks and there's Dad rounding the corner like a home stretch.

Teddy lunges.

Jacob takes off.

And his knees knock.

And he's down and scrambling *k-chunk* goes Teddy's chain the teeth gnashing but Dad's got a wrist in each hand, heaves Jacob across the rest of the lawn and up and hoofs him in the arse, *Get* inside.

Teddy goes nuts.

Right, you fucken mutt, that's it.

Dad!

Inside, I said. Inside!

Jacob runs round the corner of the apartment building, ducks back and watches. Dad's at Chuck's door, pounding. Can pound all he likes, Chuck's probably down at the Rivvy getting bombed. Dad grabs an empty from the piles either side of the door, heaves it at Teddy, but misses. Starts across the street. Jacob's up the stairs through the door and in the kitchen, waiting for it.

Here he comes.

Look at me. I said *look* at me. Smartarse, eh? Saw the car was gone.

Where is it?

In the *fucken* shop never mind. What did I tell you?

Never to go over there.

Why?

Because that dog's mad and – but he *isn't*, Dad, he's –

Get them up.

He's a good dog!

Get them up, I said!

Jacob puts his head down. Holds his hands out either side, palms up. Breathes deep. Looks up.

Dad grits his teeth but his chin's wobbly and he almost whispers I do not fucking understand you, boy, do you want to fucking *die?*

Jacob shakes his head and starts to say I'm sorry, but Dad waves him off and goes to his room. Tries to slam the door but can't because it's made of such light crappy wood.

Every day for three days Jacob cleans something different, even the cupboards, so Dad can study, but he says Fucksakes, son, enough. Smells like a bloody morgue in here.

Smells like lilacs at Neily's house. Lilacs and leather, from all the old books he has everywhere in shelves that go the whole way up to the ceiling. But even though Neily gave Dad a break on the fees for the divorce and got him into running and all, Jacob's not sure how they stayed friends. They always argue about Tories and trade unions. Listen to me, Waldengarden, if you'd worked a real fucken day in your life you'd *ach*. And if Dad gets into Neily's cognac he sometimes has night hisses about him – English *prick*, you. But still tells Jacob If you're no going to be a doctor, son, then law's a pretty close second, and either way – he taps his temple – that man'll help you develop your *mind*.

Neily's house is upstairs and his office is downstairs and when his secretaries are gone but Neily's lawyering down in Cobourg or someplace, Jacob pokes round. Runs his fingers over the fancy gold writing on the sign – Cornelius Allan Waldengarden, Barrister, Solicitor, Notary Public – breathes in the smell of the burgundy leather chair, the huge big desk. Reads bits of books but just the normal ones made out of paper. And he plinks the piano in Neily's living room. Changes channels with his flicker. When Neily's home he shows Jacob art books about Miró and Magritte, Delacroix and Dali. Neily saw some of the real paintings in Paris because he goes there all the time. And his new dog's name is Evelyn but when Jacob asks Isn't that a girl's name, Neily says It's after Evelyn Waugh, the novelist – he was a man. In the mornings they all go for jogs through the park – no hills, no intervals, just enough to keep Jacob primed and ready.

And it's the best time for the park. *Green*. And the temperature – just right. Neily's in pretty good shape except he has a playboy lifestyle and huffs a bit, but Jacob doesn't even feel winded. The *fartlek*, the intervals, the hills – they worked. Jacob knows he's ready. He knows that he's fast. When he wants to be. But it's the wanting. How much someone like Spielman or Billy Mutton wants not just to win but to beat other people bad.

Jacob, Jacob, says Neily, I'm telling you right now, big boy, there's no way you can lose. And he barbecues up a whole half chicken with his homemade sauce. Sprays water, *hiss*, on the grill and holds up his wineglass and says You'll be basking in the sun and sucking on chicken bones with a medal around your neck while everyone else is still competing. It'll be a great day.

And, the night before Brighton, when he's lying in the comfy big bed and Evelyn's down at his feet, Jacob believes Neily sort of. Sees himself winning, sitting back, sun in his face, and Dad will pass his EMCA. Get on full-time. Benefits. A plan. They could buy any books they wanted and maybe Dad'd finally be able to visit Scotland and take Jacob with him. It's only two days but Jacob aches in his belly when he thinks of Dad and how Neily's so smart but Dad feels dumb. Except he isn't. Ambulance drivers are just as important as lawyers and they should get paid the same.

Jacob pushes Evelyn off the edge of the bed and whispers Go on, lie down. Evelyn's claws *tik-tak-tik* on the wooden floor, and he snuffles and yawns and gives himself a shake. Plunks down and closes his eyes. I have to sleep, too, Jacob whispers, and he makes prayer hands on his forehead. Breathes into his belly. Wakes up in the awful hush when he has dreams of running the same turn over and over all mixed up with Teddy and Evelyn fighting, their teeth gnashing and crashing and Cailan is watching and screaming *Stop!* Evelyn gets away but one back leg is dangling by shreds and Cailan cries and cries but no one ever comes. Jacob looks through the dark but Evelyn's gone so he sits down at the end of the bed, fists under his chin, until the birds start singing.

He lies and says Super when Neily asked if he slept well. Tired, tired in his bones. But Neily's shower has massage and the smell of his shampoo makes your eyebrows bob. Plus grapefruit juice and some cheese and cold cuts, and Neily guns the Prelude with the sunroof open. They're a bit late. All the other kids are on the bus and Mr. Kazinski's waiting outside with his clipboard. Thank you for gracing us with your presence.

Sorry.

Fancy car.

My dad's friend. He's a lawyer.

Nice sweat suit, too.

My dad lent it.

Spielman sticks his head out the window and says Let's go, superstar, and Mr. K slaps Jacob's arse just when he jumps up the steps. The chicken Neily wrapped in foil bounces around in Jacob's Adidas bag and you can smell the sauce.

Jacob says Hello there to Mr. Cooper the bus driver. He just grunts. Jacob looks for a seat but keeps his eyes off Spielman, he's sitting at the back and staring at Jacob, Jacob can feel it. Dean's in long and high jump, the one and two hundred. Will probably take firsts in at least two of them. Has his arm round Melissa, who can really go in the four by one hundred even though she smokes. She doesn't give Jacob a dirty look for the first time in a long time, but she doesn't exactly smile and say Peace be with you, either. Jacob pretends not to notice, looks around at the rest of the students who gab and blab and have AC/DC or Aerosmith going on ghetto blasters.

Hey, Jacob.

It's Cracks.

Sit yo honky ass here.

He's behind Vaughan Rundle – no wonder Jacob couldn't see him, Vaughan's gotta be pushing two hundred pounds now and sweats when he eats, but can toss a shot put like stink. Asalamalakim, Cracks says, but looks at his shoes when Jacob sits down. His dad made him get another crewcut. Head like a toilet brush.

Quiet, kiddies, says Mr. K, then he does a head count. After he goes by, Jacob asks Cracks if he's all right. Dyno-mite, he says, but he doesn't sound too dynamite. Jacob knows they won't be saying much for the rest of the trip, and remembers way back in kindergarten when they held hands on their way into the Shrine Circus.

Okay, kiddies, says Mr. Kazinski up at the front of the bus when Mr. Cooper fires her up, can you turn those things down, please? Thank you. Stereos and similar nonsense will be left on the bus, and I know I don't have to remind you that you will behave yourselves accordingly. You are athletes. And you are there to win –

Everybody goes Yeah woo ballyhoo.

– with *grace*, says Mr. Kazinski.

Booo!

Lose with equal grace. Remember, you are ambassadors of Immaculate Conception and Glanisberg. Mr. Kazinski throws a look at Vaughan, who drank a mickey of Crown Royal with some other guys at last year's meet and then puked. Everybody laughs except Mr. Cooper who gives everyone that look in his big mirror and grinds her into first. Spielman says Ford means Found On Road Dead, then turns up 'Hell's Bells.'

Jacob shuts his eyes. Doesn't open them until the sign that says Brighton 5 km.

Almost there, brotha.

I can read.

And Jacob imagines the starting line. The gun. The air stretched tight like a tendon. He breathes slow and steady, then Spielman's ghetto blaster comes crashing up the aisle when the bus shudders like it hit something and steam starts coming out its nose. Mr. Cooper says *Jeez*-uss H, and grinds her into neutral. Coasts into the Shell station right by the Brighton turn. Jacob grabs Cracker's wrist and looks at his watch – 8:25 – just when Spielman picks up his ghetto blaster and says Fucken thing's *busted*.

Siddown, says Mr. Kazinski. *All* of you, for crying out loud, relax.

But Mr. K doesn't look too calm either.

And Mr. Cooper gives him a look, says You better call ahead, Ron. She's a goner.

Brighton sends down a spare bus, but by the time they get there Mr. Kazinski's moustache makes an upside down U, and everybody goes quiet when Jacob thumps the roof. He could punch right through it he's so happy, but he makes like it's the end of the world.

After Mr. K gets everyone off and goes to sort out who missed what, he comes back to the bus and says Sorry, buddy.

Jacob just shrugs. What, he asks, was the winning time?

Ten forty-eight.

Pretty good.

You're better. You were a shoo-in.

My Dad'll be steamed, Mr. K.

Hey, you tell him to come talk to me. What could we do?

Not much.

Exactly not much. This wasn't your fault, Jacob, and I'm sorry.

'Sokay.

Jacob wanders off. Lets the smile he's been hiding come out like sun. He feels light, like he could almost fly, like he could run back to Glanisberg if he had to as long as it was by himself instead of round and round in a pack with a stupid number pinned to him.

Rest of the morning he wanders around, has a look at the teams from schools with real uniforms and everything. Kids from places like Cobourg, in Prussian blue, and Uxbridge, British Racing Green – they don't look like kids from Glanisberg. They look better. Like Spielman except with more moxie. And stronger, faster. Most kids from Glanisberg who make Regionals get creamed. The winners are so happy and they deserve it for slogging it out down what their Sterling Road is, but Jacob can't help watching the losers, like this girl from Carrying Place, it's even smaller than Glanisberg and her shoes are just old North Stars, here she comes twenty yards back but still chugging it, still trying so hard it almost makes you cry. Bunch of Cobourg boys jogging by on a warm-up point and have a laugh at her. Jacob turns and takes off full licks after them, *whoosh* in his ears.

Who's *that* guy?

Thirty yards past, Jacob turns and sprints back at them. Right at them. Sticks out an elbow.

Fuck you, fag.

But Jacob just smiles over his shoulder and keeps on going. Right back to the parking lot. Glanisberg's bus is back. Mr. Cooper's just sitting there in the driver's seat, chin in his hand, staring out the window like the other side's a long time ago. Jacob jumps up the steps. D'you put all our bags back on this bus, Mr. Cooper?

He jerks his thumb to the back.

Thanks.

He just nods.

But when Jacob gets back to the front, Mr. Cooper holds his hand up, says Hang on a sec. Digs in his pocket. Hands Jacob fifty cents. Get yourself somethin to drink.

Brought water.

Something good. Pop machines in that school. Fanta and all.

You want something, Mr. Cooper?

He shakes his head. Sorry we couldn't make it.

That's okay. Really.

Been nice to see you win.

Jacob shrugs.

How's your dad keepin?

He's okay. Was gonna come today but he has his EMCA tests. For the ambulance.

Tell him I say hi.

'Kay. Thanks again, Mr. Cooper.

Inside Brighton High, Jacob follows the smell of french fries. Finds the cafeteria. The pop machine has Tahiti Treat and everything, but nothing happens when he puts his money in. He keeps pressing the button, feels eyes on him, his face heating up. Then he makes a Fonz fist like Spielman and thumps the machine. Holy jumpin, two cans?

First one's down before he even gets back outside. Then he finds a good spot way away from the track and the crowds and the noise. Plunks himself down, takes the half chicken from his bag. Unwraps the foil. Sniffs. Rips the leg off and bites into it. Tells himself to go slow but he can't it's so good. Swallows big chunks. Burps and has a look for where to wipe his hands and sees Mr. Kazinski's shoes. Then his legs, his face and his moustache like a whiplash when he says Bad timing, sport.

What do you mean, sir?

The eight-hundred's coming up.

So?

You're in it.

No I'm not. Graham Hollings–

Mr. Kazinski steps to the side and points like a game show host. There's Cracker, dead ahead under the bleachers, heaving.

Mr. Kazinski laughs and says *You* can puke *after* the race.

Jacob swallows burn, shakes his head. No way, sir.

Now's your chance, Jacob.

Not my distance, Mr. K.

Two laps?

Get Spielman to do it.

Dean's high-jumping. You're our sub, Jacob. You're it.

Jacob's jaw twitches. Can, can I stretch?

Mr. Kazinski snaps out his arm and looks at his watch. Fifteen minutes to start, he says, I'll meet you trackside in ten.

Okay, says Jacob, but his voice cracks.

By the way, says Mr. Kazinski when he's walking away backwards, Billy Mutton's running this baby, too. Then he winks and turns and jogs toward the track.

Jacob sticks his left leg out, folds his right one back, rests his forehead on his knee. Tries to focus – one, one thousand – on the count, but his hamstring shakes like a fibrillating heart.

Jesus. Billy Mutton isn't five feet nothing anymore. Almost has a moustache. Thicker legs, too. Look at the bastard. Jump squats. Shaking out his arms, nodding his head shoulder to shoulder. Wanting it.

Jacob doffs his sweatsuit and tries to fold it neat. But he's shaking. You all right, kiddo? says Mr. K.

Jacob runs on the spot – *phooh phooh phooh* – shakes out his arms, nods.

Just lock in right behind him, sport, don't give up, and use those legs of yours to get him in the stretch. Sure you're okay?

Jacob burps bone smell.

And Mr. K laughs. Go get 'im, tiger, he says, and smacks Jacob one on the butt.

Jacob gets his number, keeps his head down, jogs to his lane. Has a quick look at Billy and then a hand – big, dark – is on his ribcage, pushing him aside. Jacob looks along the long arm up to a shoulder like a shot put, and black black hair. Over the shoulder, Jacob sees Billy's eyes widen, too. This guy is taller than Jacob, taller than anyone at Immaculate Conception. Looks like the guys bused into Glanisberg High from the reservation. Except for his eyes. And the Indians at Glanisberg High don't have muscles like his either. This guy could be in comics. PJVI, says his singlet. Where is that guy from? says Jacob when he settles in beside Billy. Billy says Who gives a fuck, but Jacob can tell he's rattled. That Billy doesn't *know* he's going to win anymore.

The starter holds his gun up and puts the bullhorn against his mouth. Rrrunners, take your marks.

Jacob gags and says I'm gonna fucken puke.

Billy spits, and –

Rrready ...

Bang. He's gone.

Five feet back of him just like that and his guts going flip flop already, Jacob cannot believe the pace. Then he hears it, *pap pap pap*, like fingers on a palm but louder. Sees the lashing black hair and *barefoot*, the guy from PJVI is running *barefoot*. And passing Jacob. And Billy. Eight, ten paces up by the time they hit two hundred.

Jacob just keeps his eyes on Billy's heels and hopes to hang on for third.

But then they round the third turn and Jacob gets a lift when he sees the clock. He's *never* been this fast. Up ahead Mr. K's windmilling his arm with Cracks right by him and they're both yelling *Go*.

Jacob digs and finds it and can't believe the split – 1:18 – but hears breathing and Jesus here's another guy right on his shoulder. Making his move. He draws even with Jacob in the second turn.

And Jacob starts to fade. Feels like he could puke or shit himself right here and now. Then he hears his name. And looks. And almost falls.

It's Dad. Standing by the line and *screaming*. C'mon, boy! Dig in! Dig in!

Jacob corrects himself, but drops to fourth.

NO! *Lift* your knees, *pump* your arms, move! Dad's right on the track. Mr. Kazinski pulls him back but Dad smacks his hand off. Cups his mouth. Screams down Jacob's lane when they round the last turn. Take 'em, Jacob, take 'em! They're fading! They're fading!

Jacob has a look and it's true. PJVI went out too hard. No kick.

Pump your *arms*, pump your *arms*!

Jacob blinks and runs for Dad, right at Dad. Hard, hard, *hard*, all spit and breath and burn. Like he could run over him. Trample him. Into bloody bits all over the bastard asshole ground.

The guy in third pulls up and Jacob blasts by. Eyes Billy.

Yes! Yes! PUMP your arms he's fading do it boy!

Chest's on *fire* but Jacob draws even. Has a look – Billy's *crying* – and he's got him.

PJVI checks his shoulder. And checks again, bug-eyed.

He's *yours*, boy, he's yours!

But it comes. And Jacob just lets it – *gwlap*, all down his chin and neck and singlet, *gwlap* – and everything goes slow and quiet, like a painting.

PJVI a blur beside him.

Jacob lets the momentum take him into the first turn, but after he stops he's all wobbly and has to drop to his knees. Keeps puking. But nothing comes up.

Second place doesn't get spaghetti parmesan. It
– along with Jacob's birthday – gets a gun. Plus dentist appoint-
ments. Coupla days after the race, the EMCA people call, and – Kid,
our fucken luck's turned! – let Dad know. He passed. Fucken
distinction and all, boyo! That's them with benefits – free OHIP
and a full dental plan. Dad calls Dr. Helfgott straight away. Gets
them both in for checkups a month down the road. Then he takes
Jacob to Canadian Tire a day early and gets him the pellet gun. The
exact one he wanted last year, a Crossman .177. Same as
Spielman's. Jacob tells the Deaner when he goes with Dad to get
flowers the next day. Nicest ones ever, and Dean even helps his
mum make the bouquet. Dad pays in cash, says I'll hear nothing
of the kind, love, when Mrs. Spielman tries to cut him a deal. He
even whistles on the way out, just like when he's in the shower.

But up at Mount Pleasant he cries for the first time ever.

For the first time ever, Jacob doesn't. Then Dad says I'm not so
sure we should come here, son.

Ever?

I mean today, your birthday.

It's both our birthdays, says Jacob, and he points his toe at the
headstone.

Birthdays are for the living, son.

That's when Jacob shuts his eyes hard, and Dad holds him by
the back of the neck. Gives it a pat and says Come on, we've to get
you a cake yet, and the bakery'll be closin. Stop it now, you're all
right.

Second place also gets your picture in the paper. Weekend after
Jacob's birthday, he and Dad are out for a light two-miler, first run
since the race, and Gordie Perkins from the *Herald* snaps them on
their way back into town. Dad's smiling so big in the photo you can

see his front tooth, and in the story – *Father, Son are Glanisberg's Flying Scots* – its says 'Jacob Richard McKnight, who turned just twelve years of age three days ago, ran a blistering 800 metres in Brighton last week, but narrowly missed a berth in the all-Ontario finals later this month. "She was a close one," says John McKnight, father of the boy. "Too close to call, if you ask me."' Before that Dad told Gordie The boy missed 'er by a *ball* hair, and you could hear Gordie laughing his head off on the phone, but he didn't put it in. Or the part about Jacob puking, even though Jacob said I did, I puked my guts out. Instead it says 'The intrepid twelve-year-old overcame stomach cramps to finish within a hair's breadth of victory.' But the story isn't even in Sports. It's on the front page, just under the big bit about improvements at the factory and the open house in July. There's a picture of the director that looks like an actor. Perfect teeth. There'll be fun for the whole family, he says. Be sure to bring the kids! Dad says You'd think we get top billing, fucksakes, not *that* bloody fruit.

Factory's pretty important, Dad.

And you're no?

Jacob shrugs, but in his room at night he looks at their picture a lot. In the background you can just see the Murph's mailbox. Jacob cuts that part out. Tapes Dad and him in his sketchbook and does a drawing next to them – like the Child of Uncertain Years from *The Anatomy Coloring Book* except he's got all his limbs and organs.

Jacob's never been too sure about shooting birds – gets all shaky if they don't die straight off – but Pete Young pays fifty cents for every starling you nail. Spielman says it's because starlings ruin the apples, everybody knows that, but Jacob thinks that old Pete just likes giving them pocket money and it's kind of a pact, if you're shooting starlings then you're not stealing apples come August. Alvy says it's not true about starlings, they actually eat the bugs that are bad for apples, and starlings being here isn't their fault, it's Shakespeare's. Spielman says that's horseshit, but Alvy shows in one of his bird books. Some bampot wanted all the birds in Shakespeare's plays to be in America, so he brought a hundred starlings over and set them free. Spielman says Who cares, but he still lets Alvy come hunting. Alvy doesn't mind it, just as long, he says, as it's only starlings. Nothing else. He doesn't shoot – doesn't have a gun – but he keeps count of all the dead ones so the money's doled out fair square. Plus he keeps the odd dead bird for himself. For dissections. *That*, says Spielman, is fucken gross, but he still asks Alvy to do a dissection outside and show them. Alvy has scalpels and scissors and the lot just like in science. They all watch him cutting a bird open and Bobby almost ralphs. Alvy shows them the heart, it's maybe the size of one of Dad's knuckles but Alvy says it's way stronger than any human's. Spielman dares Bobby to eat it.

You eat it.

Give ya five bucks.

Bobby has a look like he's thinking about it, but almost ralphs again and runs away.

Alvy goes to toss the massacred bird in the bushes this side of the barbed-wire fence, but Spielman says No, keep going.

Sure?

Yeah. It's kind of inneresting.

Alvy shows them the shoulder muscles for flying. He says if we had muscles like birds then we'd be like superheroes. For such little creatures they're ultra-strong, but they have hollow bones. Not having teeth and large bones like we do also keeps them light for flying, but their sternum – Alvy calls it a carina – is big because of the stresses flying creates, and that's why they have fused collar-bones that we call the wishbone. Alvy cuts right down to it. Jacob blinks and shakes his head. Remembers the sensation of flight. The snap.

Turns out Alvy's bro studies ornithology, which comes from the Latin for *knowing birds. Birds* in Scottish English is *women*. Spielman brings bird magazines one time. Tells Bobby that he can't look, he didn't eat the heart.

So! You didn't either!

My magazines, whaleface.

Bobby goes and sits under an apple tree with his arms crossed. The rest of them have a look, and Spielman says My boner's pointin north right fucken now.

So's is mine, says Cracker.

Then Spielman says he's gonna do it right on the woman, and gets his wang out. Jacob says Are you nuts?

What? No one around.

And Spielman does it, he starts pulling the goalie right there in the orchard. Cracks, too. Alvy watches like it's science, but Jacob goes over to the fence, stares at a blue jay that lands in a little tree just the other side. Jacob knows he is not seminal yet plus Spielman would just say something about his dick wearing a turtleneck.

The blue jay, mean-looking beak, flies off, and Jacob looks back. Cracks and Spielman are yanking like no tomorrow and Alvy says It's a race! The Cracker's in the final turn! But Spielman is coming on strong, it's gonna be a close one fo–

Shut up, Chatwin, says Dean, and he puts his head down. Grits his teeth. Shuts his eyes.

Cracker's knees buckle and he says Wo ... *whoa.*

But Spielman wins.

Dissect that, Chatwin.

No *thank* you.

Jacob can't get over to the orchard as much as the other guys because of running and because he has to sneak. Uses Cracks' hockey bag to carry his gun in because if Dad found out he's shooting birds then he'd thrash him. Target practice is what that gun's for, son, a gentlemanly art, like boxing. Jacob nods, gentlemanly.

Couple weeks before school's out Dad buys a piece of plywood and a thick sheet of Styrofoam. Glues them together, and with Jacob's Prismacolors draws four plate-sized targets on the wood.

Now, I know I told you, no loaded guns inside, but we've no yard, so the kitchen it is. Only – only – when I am here are you to use this gun, do you understand?

Understand, Dad.

They practice every night when Dad isn't working. No, son, you're jerkin the trigger. Give it here. Watch now, watch. Nestle it in here, like this. Lay the cheek right along. Now, slowly raise the barrel, you just want the tip of that nib between your sights. Inhale. Then, slowly exhaling, you *squeeze* the trigger.

Jacob's scalp gets prickly when he watches Dad's left eyelid, twitching, the right eye open like murder.

Bumpf. Whap.

Bull's eye.

Dad eyes his shot and his lips make a thin dark line as Jacob imagines a Cypriot soldier dropping like a bird from a tree.

Dad?

Yeah.

When you were in Cyprus, did you –

Never mind all that. Now, your turn. Do it like I told you.

Jacob loads a pellet. Pumps the gun.

Just twice now, Dad reminds him, I'm telling you, any more's too powerful for this distance.

Jacob raises the gun, can smell Dad's after shave on the stock when he inhales. Slowly exhales. Squeezes.

Bumpf.

Dead *on*, son. Excellent. You been practicing when I'm no here?

No.

Right, see if you can do that twice in a row then. Just aim for the same hole. Odds are you won't hit it, but you'll group beautifully is the idea. That's the sign of a marksman.

Were you a marksman?

First fucken class, boyo.

What does that mean?

See out that windae?

Yeah.

Go on and look. Past your school. See the fence?

That far?

Kid, in the Black Watch I coulda put *two* in a man from here.

One week to go until Grade Seven is over, and Dad's on afternoons. Jacob's up by three birds.

Ho-lee mutha, my man, you be shootin *bad*.

My dad's helping me. He's a marksman.

Heethe a markthman, says Spielman, who missed his last two shots. And Alvy says Why are you always so mad when anyone else does good?

Shut up.

You shut up.

Spielman points his gun right at Alvy. What did you say?

You heard me.

Whoa, says Cracks, *whoa*.

And Spielman lowers his barrel.

Then nobody says anything. But nobody goes, either. They keep walking, looking, walking, looking.

Where the fuck, says Dean, are they all?

But nobody answers. Dean shoots a tree. He did not do superlatively on his English final, and unless Miss Richardson's generous, he might flunk. Alvy got exempted from everything, and Jacob, too, except for math. Cracker got exempted from everything except geography – even though he talks the dude lingo, he can write, says Miss Richardson, with both exactitude and flair. Alvy says maybe they should do a comic book together, it would be like *Power Man* or *Black Lightning* except Cracker's alter ego could be a white kid who got left in Harlem by a poor mother like with Moses. His black mother loves him hard, but all his brothers and his brothers' friends beat the crap out of him until one day when he's hiding in a trash can down an alley he finds the sacred lost amulet of –

Can I be in it? says Bobby.

Shut up, says Spielman, and everybody looks at where he's pointing his gun.

Don't, says Alvy, but Spielman takes a bead.

And pegs the blue jay right in the head.

They all walk up to it slow, slow, and look.

Everyone shut up, says Spielman.

But nobody's saying anything.

Spielman picks it up by a wing, starts walking to the fence.

Leave it, says Alvy.

Wanna cut it up? Here, have it. Spielman chucks the bird at Alvy. And holy fuck, Alvy goes for Spielman like a grounder and dives right into his legs. Spielman's gun goes flying and Cracker yells Break it up, but it's too late for that. Alvy and Spielman are all tangled together and rolling. Then Spielman screams and Alvy rolls off, and up, and he's running. Spielman's on his knees and holding his forearm. He *bit* me, little faggot *bit* me. Jacob screams Go, Alvy, and Spielman all teeth fires him a look. Then *bang* he's gone and gaining on Alvy like a greyhound. Jacob goes hard, but Spielman got the head start, and he's on Alvy's ass in heartbeats.

The little guy doesn't stand a chance this time.

Dean's got him pinned stomach down. Fucken *girl*, fucken *bite* me? Eh?

Get *off* me, my back! Jacob!

Dean gets a handful of hair. Rams Alvy's head. Looks at Jacob. Rams it again, and Alvy's face, his mouth's wide open but no sound's coming out, just spitstring hanging between his lips. Then he breathes like he was just born, and bawls Help me.

Bite *me*, you fucken asshole?

Jacob goes for Dean.

Yanks his arms back – Get off him! – but Spielman gets one arm free just when Alvy rolls and *twok* he clocks him. Right on the jaw. Alvy rolls up and runs all bent with both hands cupping his face and Spielman twists round and shoves Jacob down. You want it, too, asshole?

Stop it, says Cracker. And Bobby's under a tree hiding his head. Jacob scoots up and runs after his friend.

Yeah, McKnight, run. Run like you always do.

Alvy!

Run run run!

Shut your garbage mouth, says Jacob over his shoulder. Alvy!

But Alvy keeps going.

Alvy. Wait!

Alvy turns and screams. Asshole!

And Jacob stops dead. Alvy, he says.

Leave me alone!

Let me look.

No! And Alvy turns, and he's crying, and he's running best his knee will let him.

Jacob drops to his knees and hammers the ground. Gets up. Walks right at Spielman. Cracks gets in between.

Get out of the way, Graham.

Gonna have to move me, Jacob.

Let him, says Spielman. I'll smash his face.

He had an oper-*a*-tion, Dean!

So what? says Spielman, and he holds up his arm and points at the teeth marks. He *bit* me.

Jacob jabs a finger at his own jaw and says You hit him right *here.*

Coulda helped him, big man.

I *did* help him, you didn't have to –

Fucken stood there and watched is what you did.

Jacob tries a slip but Cracker bear-hugs him. Just go, Jacob, he'll murder you.

Jacob shakes – Lemme go – free, and says All right, I'm going. You coming, Cracks? But Cracks just stands there. Bobby, you coming? But Bobby has his head down behind his arms. Shakes it. And Spielman puts his hands on his hips, and his stupid face says *See?* And he laughs when Jacob gets his gun and runs. All the way back to where their bikes are.

Alvy's long gone.

And Jacob's forgotten Cracks' bag. Screw him, anyway. He takes side streets, but keeps his eye out for the ambulance – you never know if Dad'll be out on a call. But he gets home okay. Stashes the gun, tells himself he's never using the stupid bastard thing ever again, then bikes by Alvy's. Sees his bike, dumped on the front lawn. Jacob dumps his and goes to bash on the door. But Mrs. Chatwin comes out. She's all dolled up and smells perfumey and before Jacob can say anything she says Honey, you best get back on your bike.

Alvy okay?

I think he'll live.

It isn't broken?

No. Wouldn't mind slapping that what's-his-name's face, though, let me tell ya.

Spielman. Dean Spielman.

That's twice now.

I know.

What's that arsehole's problem?

I tried to get in there and stop him but –

It's all right, Jacob. But you best just give Alvy a couple of days. Let him cool down.

Okay.

Okay.

You look nice, Mrs. Chatwin.

Yeah. Well. So much for my big plans. Back in she goes, and Jacob picks up his bike, swings his leg over and *bam*, he looks and it's Alvy at an upstairs window. Smacking it with a bag of frozen peas. Jacob shouts I'm sorry, but Alvy slams his middle finger against the glass. Then disappears.

And he's not at school the next day. Or the next.

At home, Jacob turns back to plates 19 and 20 in *The Anatomy Coloring Book*, the bones of the skull. Can't remember now when he coloured them, even though temporal means time. He did the mandible all in gold like the face plate of Iron Man's helmet. He's not really sure where Alvy got operated on, but he flips ahead to the Child of Uncertain Years, says Sorry, and flips back to Plate 19. Chooses Cobalt Green, because that's going to be Arsenal's armour, and lightly colours over the gold. The combination, it almost vibrates.

Alvy's back at school the next day, but he keeps his head down and stays away from everyone. In gym Jacob fakes a limp and tells Mr. Kazinski he might have strained his patellar ligament.

Seen someone?

No, but I'm pretty sure. Been hittin the hills with my Dad. Puts a lot of stress on the patellar region.

Thank you, doctor. Why don't you join Sulky Sue over there and exercise your drawing skills? Rest of you bums, four laps of the field and don't let me hear any bellyaching!

Spielman and Cracks lead the pack, and Jacob goes over to where Alvy's sitting with his sketchbook. He's drawing the Hulk.

How's it going, guy? Jacob sits down, Alvy shrugs.

I don't get why you won't even just talk.

Alvy looks straight ahead.

Jacob puts a hand on his shoulder.

Alvy lets it sit for a sec, then shrugs it off.

C'mon, Alvy.

He points his pencil at his scar and says It still hurts, you know.

I bet it does.

That throwback asshole, he hit me there on *purpose.*

I know he did. I know. But why are you staying mad at me?

You know why.

Alvy, I tried, I tried to get him off you.

Yeah, right.

Hey. See you, Chatwin. And Jacob stands, way over him, thinks about hoofing that sketchbook out of Alvy's lap and saying Fight your own battles, wimp. But that would be like stomping on a flower, a little baby bird, so he just starts sprinting after the pack. Eyes Spielman and Cracker. He's gonna catch them. Gonna run circles round every-damn-body.

Hey, Hermes, says Mr. Kazinski through cupped hands, what about that knee?

Over his shoulder Jacob shouts I don't feel a thing.

But he rips out Plate 19 that night and tosses it right in the trash. Wolfs down a meat pie and goes to bed, no teeth brushed, way early. Tosses. Turns. Finally sleeps.

Until Dad kicks the bed frame so hard the mattress falls off and Jacob's still blinking and giving his head a shake when Dad has him by the back of the neck *Get* out here. And his breath stinks of it and Jacob's brain beehives with what's it he's forgot the garbage the dishes left the oven on? Dad shoves him to the middle of the kitchen, his eyes shut against the light *Look* at me, and *bam*, he's down.

Up.

Jacob's holding his ear with one hand and trying to pull himself across the floor with the other when the guts drop out of him. It's the gun. Someone's seen him. Someone's seen it and someone's finked.

I said *up.*

Jacob grabs corners of the oven, pulls himself up. Puts his head down.

Look at me.

Jacob looks. Dad's face is murder. Are you fucking stupid, boy?

Jacob stares at floor.

Answer me. Are you fucking stupid?

Jacob shakes his head.

No? You're no? Did you no think I would see this?

It was just for money, Dad, so I could save up something for your birthday.

You asked her for money?

Jacob looks at Dad. He takes a folded-up piece of paper from his back pocket, holds it up *snap*. Know what this is?

No.

Oh, you don't? You're not stupid. Go on, have a guess.

I don't know, says Jacob, but his chin wobbles.

This, says Dad, is a fucking telephone bill. Now, I want you to come here and look. Get over here and look. See here, smartarse? *This* is what tells you the long-distance calls you made. Now, who's number would that be?

Dad it was just ten seconds –

Whose number is it?

Mum's I hung up –

Bam on the other ear.

I don't fucken care how long it was. What have I telt you? *What* have I telt you?

Never to call her.

Why?

Because she doesn't –

Give. A. *Damn*, boy. Dad says it foul-breathed right in Jacob's face.

I know, Dad. I hung up.

What's this about you askin for money?

I didn't, I didn't, Dad, I swear. It wasn't even ten seconds. A man –

Eh?

A man answered and I hung up.

What did he say?

Nothing. Just hello and I hung up.

You havin me on, boy?

No, Dad, I swear. I didn't even say hello.

Dad's hand, the one holding the bill, drops to his side. The other one's a fist, but he just presses it 'gainst his temple and paces, stops by the window. Stares. Go on to your bed, he says.

It's busted.

Jesus suffer fuck, says Dad. Then he crumples the bill and throws it against the window. Stomps into Jacob's room. Yanks and jerks and bashes the frame apart, stands the pieces in the corner. Squares the mattresses on the floor. Sweat racing down his face. Breathing hard. *In*, he says, and don't come out. Shuts the door behind him.

Jacob lies flat on his back, eyes wide, heart thumping. Dad, in the kitchen, out the kitchen. Ice, cracking. Jacob crawls quiet as he can till his head's at the foot of the bed. Listens and listens. Just the TV and, across the road, Teddy, barking and barking. Chuck must be home, and Teddy wanting fed, with nothing but dirty water in his bowl.

Jacob opens his eyes. Blinks and listens, listens and blinks. He's not dreaming it. It's real. Up out the bed he runs *pap pap pap* through the kitchen. Stops outside Dad's bedroom door just in case. Peeks. Empty. Jacob ducks round Dad's bed to the window. It's Dad and Chuck on the stoop, and – Jacob presses his cheek against the glass – Teddy at the end of his chain, barking growling gnashing 'cause Dad's got hold of Chuck now, and he's bashing him about the ears. Slapping his face.

Jacob cracks the window an inch, two.

Will you or won't you?

Get the fuck away –

Slap slap bang, Pardon me?

Sorry, fuck.

I fuckingwell hope you are. Now are you gonnae do it, or is it me? 'Cause I will. I will do it right the fuck now in front of you.

Lemme go, fuck. I'll get it.

You better fuckingwell get it, I'm standing right here till you do.

Chuck goes inside and Jacob ducks away from the window when Dad turns round and folds his arms on his chest. Jacob backs up. Climbs on Dad's bed. Hunkers down on all fours. Has a look just when – *Jee*-zuss – Chuck comes out with his .22.

And hands it to Dad.

He pats the back of Chuck's neck, says something that Jacob can't hear because Teddy's going nuts now.

Dad opens the chamber. Checks. Walks to the edge of the stoop. Kneels –

No, Dad.

Aims.

Bang.

And there's no more barking.

Dad steps off the stoop, and Jacob jumps off the bed. Whole side of his face smushed against the glass, he can just see Teddy. Down. Shaking everywhere like electrocution. Dad cocks the gun, puts his foot on Teddy's ribs, the barrel behind an ear, and fires. Walks safe with the gun back to Chuck. Chuck has to hold himself up against the wall. Dad squeezes his arm, says something in his ear. Chuck shakes his head, and Dad leans the gun against the house. Starts crossing the street.

The breath heaving out of him, Jacob smooths the bed. Runs back to his room and dives under the covers. Tries to breathe slow, slow, slow when Dad comes up the stairs heavy, heavy, heavy. And just stands in the kitchen breathing, breathing, breathing. Jacob stuffs knuckles in his mouth but can't stop the sound, but Dad doesn't come in. Whacks open the kitchen cupboard, spins the cap and hauls it straight from the bottle.

Chuck Linton's old flatbed turns over. Going to bury him, Jacob thinks, or just toss him in the river or some ditch somewhere. He curls and bites harder and knocks, knocks, knocks his head against his knees.

Dad takes another haul and says Showed you, cunt. But then he gags, and asks for mercy.

THREE

The new place, out back the Riverbend Restaurant, is bigger than at Hillcrest Heights, but it smells like garbage. And grease. Tommy Kwan, the landlord, says Ventilation I fix, plus he gives Dad deals on frozen turkey. And the deck's big. Except seagulls shit all over it. They're always around, screaming at each other and trying to get at the Riverbend's garbage, stinking heaps of fat black bags in blue bins under the deck. Jacob takes a stool out sometimes, likes the watching the river and the swallows, amazing flyers, dive-bombing the gulls. Filthy birds.

Could peg any one of you bastards at thirty paces.

But Jacob's Crossman stays where it is – in the closet with all the boxes Dad never unpacks when they move.

Dad's been all right, though, since he saw Jacob's final report card. Got a C and a B this year. The rest was all A. Miss Richardson wrote in Comments that Jacob faced difficulties this year, but he overcame them admirably. He is an excellent student, but his talents require careful guidance. Promoted to Grade Eight! Dad said a little knowledge is a dangerous thing, but after spaghetti parmesan and a couple Goldens he said Jimmy, bring the boy some baklava, he's a bloody fucking genius, don't you know.

And he's looking at canoes, too. Brand-new ones in Canadian Tire.

Pretty expensive, Dad.

Ach, summer and all. But he tells the clerk he'll give it some thought and taps his temple.

Meantime, Neily Waldengarden has them down to his house for dinners outside. Says he's sorry he missed Jacob's races. Second in Regionals – by a ball hair, Johnny, by a ball hair – and puking up my famous chicken deserve a summer of conciliatory celebrations. Conciliatory comes from Latin for *to combine or unite physically*. Down at Neily's it's top-drawer. He teaches Jacob how to toss a tight spiral, and they run plays with Dad in the huge big yard. Neily nicknames Dad Paddles because of his hands, the ball always bounces off them, but Dad blames Evelyn for getting in the way. Then they sit down for big feeds. Barbecue chicken and ribs. Potato salad and corn on the cob except Jacob can tell how it hurts Dad's teeth even just to chew it. Then if there's no football on, Dad and Neily have a go about Trudeau and trade unions or the IRA. Johnny, Johnny, you're being irrational. See you who's never been down a mine or held a fucken gun in your hands. That's when Neily breaks out the cognac and patches it up with Dad over backgammon while Jacob plays fetch with Evelyn. Evelyn Waugh wrote *A Handful of Dust*, and Neily says Jacob can have it, he's got two copies.

It's all top-drawer, really it is, but Plague has invaded the City of the Living with his radioactive zombie minions. And he has created a monster, a new servant he names Decay who used to be a good guy and would have been a superhero except he got in a fight with X-Calibre about who should be the leader of the Living. Arsenal was out on patrol when it happened and couldn't help, so he who became Decay won and stole X-Calibre's power gun. Without it, X-Calibre is mostly helpless until he can make a new one, so it's Arsenal all alone against the armies of darkness. The fight of his life. But Plague and Decay won't even show themselves yet. They're wearing Arsenal down. And something is wrong with his armour. He can fight and fly only half the time he used to before his energy crystals wear down. X-Calibre hooks him up to machines and tries to figure out the problem while he's also trying to build a new power gun. I need *time*. We don't *have* time, blast you. Arsenal can't keep going. He doesn't want to fight zombies every day forevermore. He wants to breathe real fresh air. He wants to go swimming naked in pure clean water. He wants to see his own face in the mirror – even if it's burned and scarred it would be better than this helmet, this cursed face plate.

Jacob gets the story easy enough, but it's the pictures that give him a hard time. The motion. Getting the bodies so they say what the words are saying, or can't say. If it was all just words, then comic books wouldn't be comic books, they'd be mostly blank. Picasso and Dali and all those guys in the library, they do wonky things with the body and everyone says it's great art, but it's the body, and how it talks, that's the toughest thing in the world to draw right. *The Anatomy Coloring Book* has helped Jacob draw better, at least better musculature, and sometimes Jacob gets the whole body bang on. But he has to start over and over and draw the exact same thing umpteen times. If everyone went around with their insides out, then Jacob could draw them perfect – lungs, heart, liver, spleen. But his superheroes usually come out like Steve Ditko's – spastic – and Alvy's, Alvy's are like Sal or John Buscema. Almost perfect. And Jacob's getting sick of just sitting inside and drawing, or going for walks round the dumb town. Cracks and the Deaner and Bobby on their bikes, towels round their necks and scuba masks on their heads, heading off to the pool or the rock quarry. But even if Bobby yells hi, Jacob pretends he didn't hear. Pretends he didn't even see them. Pretends he's invisible.

Until one day, when July's almost half-over, he and Dad turn in a fast six, and he feels really good, and light, and right after his shower he says Bugger it, and bikes down to Becker's. Buys toffee, gobstoppers plus two Bar Sixes, and bikes up to Alvy's. Summer is too short not to conciliate.

The house looks dead. Brown grass. And all the flowers Mrs. Chatwin planted have gone humpbacked, and wrinkly like foreskins. Jacob knocks like the whole place might fall if you hit it any harder.

Hello?

He tries a little harder.

Mrs. Chatwin?

He backs up, megaphones his hands. Alvy! Nothing.

Gets back on his bike. Hits the brakes when he hears the door. Freezes when he sees Mrs. Chatwin. Her face. Like it's preserved in a jar. But Jacob pretends not to notice. Dumps his bike and smiles and says Hello there.

Mrs. Chatwin just stares. Her eyes have beer bellies.

Is Alvy home?

She blinks like a hypnotist just snapped his fingers. Runs a hand through her scraggly hair.

Jacob walks a little closer, but keeps his distance. Can smell it from here. Is, he says, Alvy home?

She shakes her head and mumbles.

His brother? Alvy's with his brother?

She nods.

In Alberta?

She nods.

Oh. Alvy didn't tell me.

Mrs. Chatwin crosses her arms, rubs her shoulders, shrugs. Didn't want to stay, she says.

When's he back?

Not sure.

He's coming back, isn't he?

Her eyes water.

Sorry, says Jacob.

Not your fault, honey. Mrs. Chatwin tries to smile, but her face folds into a frown instead.

If Alvy calls can you tell him Jacob says hi?

Sure will, handsome.

And hopes he comes back to Ontario real soon.

Okay, Jacob, says Mrs. Chatwin, nodding, holding it back.

Sorry, says Jacob again, but Mrs. Chatwin doesn't hear him because she's coughing like a bone's caught in her throat. Waves him off when he walks a little closer.

He tries to pedal fast, faster, faster, down Bridge Street hill, but the chain falls off and he has to stop with his feet. Gets off and slams the bike on the ground. Could toss the crappy old thing right in the river.

Getting dark, and Dad won't be home from the hospital until midnight, but Jacob's still shaky when he takes the slice of bread. Tears it into bits, scatters them across the far end of the deck. Tries to whistle like Dad, sharp and high. Can't. Licks his lips, tries again. Spit and air. He goes back in. Opens the closet door.

Digs it out.

Loads a pellet.

Just one, he says. And if you miss, then stop.

He pumps the gun. Once, twice. And again. For insurance.

Takes one of the stools out, puts the gun across his knees. Shivers.

Gulls hover. Scream.

Jacob raises his gun. Aims.

But a swallow catches his eye, swooping banking skimming the river's surface.

And another settles on the patio railing. *Chirp.*

Get, says Jacob. Go *on.* Jacob waves with the barrel. I said get.

Hop hop, *chirp.*

You stupid, little bird? Get out of here. Jacob points the gun, says I'm telling you.

Chirp, hop.

Thwap.

No!

A sudden red dot in the plump white chest. The bird flap flap flaps but falls to the deck, where it hops and screams and screams and hops. Blood filling its bill.

Jacob drops the gun. Bangs open the door. Trips into the kitchen. Looks, looks – Help me, he says – and grabs a cereal bowl. Fills it at the sink. Dashes back out, and sets the bowl near the bird. Like the water is holy and will heal. Here, little bird, here. But it hops and screams and blood drips, drips, drips from the overflowing bill. Jacob's heart hammers and he says I'm sorry I'm sorry I didn't mean to.

But he knows what he has to do.

Spills B Bs into his shaking hand and all over the floor back in the kitchen. Loads the gun and pumps it five times. Back on the deck his whole body quakes. Poking, missing, poking, he finally pins the bird with the barrel.

Bumpf.

The little claws *scrape-scrape-scrape* and it rolls and flutters and opens its beak wide.

Bumpf.

And Jacob swallows burn.

Picks the bird up by the tip of its wing, and tosses it in the river. Screams at the gulls. Get away!

And looks at the bloody mess.

Again and again, his arms shaking and shaking, Jacob comes back from the sink with bowlfuls. Splashes the deck. One little bird. So much blood.

Arsenal didn't mean it. He was mad with X-Calibre, he was furious with him for inventing the suit of armour in the first place, for imprisoning him, but it was the armour's fault – the circuitry, it went haywire. But he'll redeem himself, he'll conciliate. He will carry X-Calibre's body in his arms and fly with him from the tower. Beyond the river. Beyond the City of the Living into the Contaminated Zone. And he'll keep flying, flying until his energy crystals run out or until he finds a secret place, a place free from radiation and zombies. An orchard, where everything's growing and you can eat right from the trees. And he will bury him there. And take off the armour.

But Jacob tears up the whole thing. His hand's still shaky, and the drawings stink.

On their last big feed down at Neily's before Dad and Jacob see Dr. Helfgott, Neily says Johnny boy, people around town will think your son is hanging out with aging homos.

Eh?

You need to get out and meet yourself a woman.

Mind the boy.

Neily takes a sip of vsop and says Just kidding, Jacob.

But Jacob starts to thinking.

Dad *has* been going out nights. Says it's just the Legion for a nip or two and a bullshit with the lads. But when he comes home he doesn't smell like the Legion. And up at the hospital cafeteria half the nurses smile with the old *double entendre* and say *Hiii*, Johnny. 'Lo, love, you're lookin well. Dad always says there is no denying the charm of a Scottish gentleman. Maybe he is screwing. Nurses in movies and tv are like mercy or libidinous, which is from the Latin for *lust*. Short dresses. White stockings. In bed Jacob listens for another body, screwing sounds. Nothing. But no night hisses, either. No prayers for mercy.

Jacob turns down the lollipop. Spends the rest of the day letting bloody cotton wads fall from his aching mouth to the toilet. Makes slow laps of the apartment. Prods his cheeks. Works his lower jaw. His tongue feels thick, useless, and he wants to ask Dad if he can skip tomorrow's run, maybe the next day's, too.

Speak the hell up, boy, I can't hear a bloody word you're saying.

Hurts to talk, Dad.

Buck up. He took all of mine not two, and you don't hear me complainin.

Jacob goes to his room, stays there. Not hungry, Dad. Just a wee bit of Bovril, son. Not hungry, Dad. Suit yourself then. He sits on the edge of his bed, pushes away the comic books he's been trying to read. The pictures look dead. Slowly he kneels beside the bed, slides the sketchbook out, but his pencils feel like extra fingers he's sprouted and hasn't learned how to use. Two days till Dad's birthday, and he still doesn't know what to draw. Could just get him another Pavarotti, and Dad would say That's great, son, really, but Jacob wants to make him something good. He's forty-two years old and doesn't even have his own teeth.

Jacob swallows blood and has to go change his wads. Dad's got the eleven o'clock news on. And a big rumsky. Ice tinkles in the glass when he points it at the TV because Pierre Trudeau makes Joe Clark look dumb again. That gormless chipmunk, says Dad, who in his right mind would vote for him?

In the washroom Jacob rinses, spits. Wipes the sink. Opens wide as he can and has a look at the holes. Fingers them. Promises to brush every day when he's better. Floss. Drink juice, not Tahiti Treat. And stay off the chocolate.

Back in the living room, Dad's snoring, neck kinked over the back of the chesterfield. Over his head, the red hackle he put up looks like it's sprouting right out the wall. In the photo beside it, Dad's in his dress uniform, big grin on his face and all his own teeth and he's pointing a Sterling machine gun at the person taking the picture. In the one on the other side he's in full battle gear. No smile. Leaves all over his helmet. Belgian FN slung over his shoulder. Bayonet fixed. Marksman, First Class.

Jacob eases the glass from Dad's hand, turns off the telly, then the light. Steals a sip, winces when it hits the holes, then rinses the rest down the kitchen sink. He has an idea, but it'll have to wait to tomorrow, when he can go to the library.

One time Mrs. Bailey took all the Judy Blume books and cut out the dirty bits. Books with big floppy gaps in them. Now she's used black marker or paper and tape to cover what she says is the filth in those art books. But *The Birth of Venus* is okay. That, she says, is art. Jacob doesn't want to argue this time. He just wants to copy that picture best he can in his sketchbook and give it to Dad. Because it's Cyprus. He read that. Where Aphrodite was born. It was just the Romans called her Venus but the Greek story came first.

Copying her takes forever. No lunch or nothing. Just gets up to swish his mouth a couple of times, and gets right back at it. My, Jacob, says Mrs. Bailey, aren't we inspired today?

I want to finish this.

Yes, I can see that.

It's my Dad's birthday tomorrow.

I see. Where's your friend?

Who?

The little noisy one.

Gone.

Ah. Well. I'll leave you to your masterpiece.

Thank you.

Jacob puts his head back down, but he can tell Mrs. Bailey's dying for a look, probably in case he's drawing pornographies. But except for one boob all her bits are covered up by her river of red hair just like in the original. Near closing time, Mrs. Bailey pretends to be putting books back on the shelves behind Jacob, but he can tell she's having a look. And he lets her.

Why, Jacob, that's, you did *very* well.

Thank you.

But what's this, here? That's not in the picture.

I know. It's my dad's shadow. From when he was in the army. On Cyprus. It's the Isle of Love because of Aphrodite, and my dad's watching her being born.

I see.

It's like a secret bursting inside of him, the picture, and Jacob can't even wait. I know it's not till tomorrow, Dad, but I made you something for your birthday.

Is that right?

Jacob nods. Wanna see?

Think I'll just wait till tomorrow.

Oh.

I'm only jokin, show us it then.

You have to close your eyes. No peeking! Ready?

Ready.

'Kay, you can open them.

What's this then?

I made it.

Very good, son.

It's *The Birth of Venus*.

I'm no dummy.

I was just –

Nice pair of tits you've given her.

Dad.

I'm allowed to notice. Dad keeps looking, Jacob waits, he sees it. What's this bit here?

That's you. See your army picture?

Which?

The one on the right. See? The shadow's like your helmet.

Dad's face scrunches.

It's Cyprus, Dad. Where Venus was born. The Isle of Love.

Isle of Love my arse. Good men died there.

Jacob stares at floor, his throat going cloggy. Thinks he should have just bought another Pavarotti or ABBA, but when he looks up, Dad's still staring at the drawing, and smiling a bit, a bit more, a bit more, till you can just see the pits in his gums.

On his real birthday, Dad's out the door early, comes home with a canoe tied to the roof and Annie tossed in the passenger side. Leaves the canoe where it is, hucks Annie inside.

What's *she* for, Dad?

What do you think she's for?

Beats me.

Boy, before you so much as *dip* a paddle in that river you're goan to learn water safety. The Kiss of Life.

On her?

'Swhat she's made for.

Dad flops Annie on the kitchen floor, spits in his hands and says Pitter patter let's get at 'er.

Now?

Got tae get her back to hospital, like.

You ripped her *off*?

See you, I borrowed her. Now, let's get goan.

Dad.

No time like the present.

Why do *I* need to know CPR? If I fell in you could do it on me.

And what about your old dad? What if he fell in the water?

You can swim.

Course I can, says Dad. But you never know what can happen. 'Sides, best you knew CPR by now, anyway.

Jacob looks at the face, at the glassy eyes, the mouth's dark hole.

'Fraid of her?

No.

Right, then. You go that side, I'll go this. Now, if it was two of us here, I'd be working on the heart and you'd be respiratin her.

I know.

Aye. Well. The blowin into her's pretty straightforward. Make sure the mouth's clear, and the lungs as well, pumping, if necessary, the legs. Like so.

'Kay.

Right. Then it's nostrils pinched, head at about this angle, and – bend down here, have a look – see me?

Yeah.

Like this, Dad says, and, covering Annie's mouth with his, breathes *phoooh*.

Jacob falls on his bum and says Holy!

What in hell's the matter?

Her chest moved!

Supposed to.

She's anatomically correct?

See for yourself, says Dad, and he nods at Annie's crotch.

Dad.

I'm only kiddin, Chrissake. Anyway. It's exactly what you want. The chest to rise, I mean. Look for it. You're filling those lungs with air until they work on their own again. Give it a go.

Jacob, heart thumping, doesn't move.

Son, your patient's dyin. Get to work.

Jacob bends over her. Tilts the head, pinches and –

Son, she's no your fucken auntie. Don't pucker up. Cover her mouth with yours and breathe.

Ha-*phooh*.

That's it.

Ha-*phooh*!

Whoa-whoa-Jesus, she's not a balloon! Breathe and pause, wait for my one and two and three and four, or, if you're alone, come back to the heart yourself, then breathe in her again, have a look and a listen, so on ... You with me?

Jacob nods.

Right then, that's no bad. Okay, Annie, thank you, love. Dad scoops her up, plunks her on the kitchen counter. She slouches, stares.

Then Dad lies down. Palms up. Cracks an eye. C'mon then, he says, you've pulled me in to shore, I'm unconscious, no phone about, what are you gonnae do?

What I did with Annie.

Get to it then. My life's passin before my eyes.

Dad, I already did it.

No quite the same. Real live specimen here.

Dad.

Chrissakes, boy, I'm not gonnae bite. Dad closes his eyes, lets his mouth sag.

Down on one knee, Jacob leans his ear to Dad's chest. Hears his heart, strong, but pretends it's barely there. Checks the pulse. Pretends it's faint. Explores the toothless mouth. Pumps Dad's legs. Kneels by his side again. Hand on hand, palm upon heart. One *and* two *and* three *and* four.

Dad cracks an eye and says Put some *umph* in it, boy.

Jacob grits his teeth. ONE and TWO and THREE and FOUR. Head tilted. Nostrils pinched, Jacob swallows, blinks.

Johnny, it's over.

Takes a big breath.

Digs if you stop I fucken swear I'll –

Shakes the bits out his head and blows till there's nothing left in his lungs.

Dad's chest swells. The heart, he whispers.

Jacob makes a fist like on *M*A*S*H* when Hawkeye's losing someone and says don't you die on me, goddammit. *Boof* in the chest.

Dad bolts up. *Fucken* hell, boy, tryin to break my ribs?

You're alive.

No thanks to you. What's with the face?

And Jacob's face, his head, his shoulders shake, and his teeth chatter like he just crawled from cold water. It's your *birth*-day, Dad.

I know that. C'mere now, you did well, son. I'm sorry, I didnae mean to scare ya.

It's your birthday, and you can't even eat anything good.

What, 'cause of my teeth, you mean?

Jacob nods on Dad's shoulder, but Dad says Teeth nothing, I'll be gettin whatever I like down me.

Jimmy's?

No. Stopped in at Sharpe's on the way home. The girls are makin us up a basket and all.

A picnic? Jacob wipes his face.

Yeah. Dad nods outside and says We'll throw that baby in the water and have a paddle round. Stop in down the park and that's us with a good nosh.

Do we have to have a portage?

A what?

When you carry it.

I'm carrying that thing as far as the water, that's it. Now, let's get her nibs back to hospital. Time we're done, our basket'll be ready.

It rains so much in July that Dad turns the canoe over on the deck and says Might have to paddle that hoor to work one day. Come August, though, the weather's brilliant and they're on the river almost every day. Now and then – *See that, Dad?* – a perch or pickerel jumps, and the odd cabin cruiser *g-glug-glugs* by, makes big waves, but it's quiet out there. Sometimes they just let her drift, and sunlight does Russian dances on the water that slooshes softly against the prow, and Dad stares way far away, tells stories that always start When I was a lad your age ...

And every week the distances down Sterling Road get a little longer. But even after eight, ten miles, at seven then six minutes per, Jacob's lungs feel deep as mine shafts, and his heart feels huge as a factory. Lot of runs alone, though, because Dad's still going out nights and getting home late. Running alone on summer mornings would be fine with Jacob except he keeps thinking he hears that car. The slobbering dog in the back. And the Murph leaning out his window. *Hey there, Runner Boy, need a ride?* But maybe he's taking the summer off from scaring the crap out of people, because every time Jacob checks his shoulder, it's just someone else, or open road. Sometimes people honk. It used to mean Get off the damn road, but now, unless they're bampots, it's more like Hey there, or even Go get 'em, kid.

When I was a lad your age, I used to run round the highlands wi' my pals and try and catch haggis.

Catch it?

Aye – pass your old dad a Golden – it's a bird, don't you know.

No it's not. Here.

Ta. It is, too.

Haggis is a stomach, Dad.

It isn't. It's a wee bird – you wantin a pop? – one leg shorter than the other. So's it can run round the highlands nae bother.

Jacob burps root beer out his nose and says That's daft.

You're daft. Dad sticks his hand in the water and *sploosh* gets Jacob.

Jacob *k-splash* gets Dad.

Then Dad shakes water out his eyes. Rocks the canoe and says That's you in, boy. And Jacob grabs each gunwale tight and yells *No*.

I'm only jokin, says Dad. He's quiet for a while. Sips his beer, says This is the life.

Tell us another one, Dad.

Eh?

Another story. When you were a bairn.

That's enough stories for today, son.

Some nights Jacob sits up and tries to picture him. With the moppy blond hair he said he had, and his wee shorts and scraped knees. Goan down the fish shop for his chips, all wrapped up in newspaper. Sharing them with a pal. But it's hard to see Dad as a bairn. Jacob keeps seeing Cailan in his place. Peas in a pod. When all Mum and Dad's British friends came down from Toronto for pahties in the summer, that's what they said: You and your boys, John, peas in a pod you are.

The next day Jacob's shaking a bit but he goes ahead and asks Dad if he remembers all that, if he remembers all the pahties and the one time when the flatbottom boat drifted in. You fixed it up but whacked your thumb with the chisel and Mum had to wrap it up until it was this big, remember? But you worked on the boat with one hand and got it all painted, and there was the sail got made with a skull and crossbones and everything. We all pretended to be pirates and sailed round the bay and fishermen yelled at us to be quiet but we didn't even care. I had a huge big cutlass, and we got scared when you told us you could hear the mermaids. Cover your ears, lads, and when we asked why, you said the mermaids would lure us to our watery graves. Cailan flipped up his patch and he kept looking over the side – remember? – and he said I *saw* one I saw one! He believed it more than Santa Claus and you never let on maybe it was just a big pickerel. Remember?

I remember.

That was fun.

So it was. Your mum made that sail.

Yeah.

The size of the thing.

It was two whole sheets!

Dad nods, and stares at the water, and Jacob wishes maybe he didn't tell the story in case Dad's remembering the night he forgot to tie up the boat. And in the morning, it was gone. They went up and down the river looking and looking. Asked fishermen. Nothing. Mum said That man, mind like a sieve, and Dad bashed the table so hard that the peas jumped off his plate. But now he just smiles and says Mermaids, and shakes his head. Those were good days, son, those were good days.

The Murph's got a knife longer than Jacob's forearm. He wipes each side on a small white towel, then slides it through the middle of a long fat watermelon. Makes triangles. Arranges them like he's an artist on the big bowls of crushed ice with chocolate bars in them, too. If it weren't for him, then the Open House would be top-drawer except when Jacob joins the lineup for hamburgers and sees them. Spielman. And Cracks. And Bobby. He puts his head down, gets his burg and root beer and walks back to where Dad's carrying on with a bunch of nurses. He got his new teeth two days ago, and he's grinning big. One of the nurses says I can't believe how much you've grown, Jacob, and Dad gives them a laugh when he says I swear that galoot's got a hollow leg, all the food goes down him. But he nods his head at Jacob as if to say G'wan and bugger off, play with your pals.

Jacob wanders round a bit, watches the egg toss and wheelbarrow race – there're prizes and the lot – then he says Bugger it, and walks on over. Bobby – It's Jacob! – sees him first. Jacob waves.

Asalamalakim.

Hey, Cracks ... hey, Dean.

But Dean just takes a bite of his burger.

We saw you, says Bobby.

In your canoe, says Cracker.

We were swimming in the sheep wash, says Bobby.

Oh.

Dig it? Cracker asks.

Dig what, says Jacob while he watches Spielman look this way, that way, chewing.

Your canoe, sucka.

My Dad bought it for his birthday. We might paddle to Hastings.

Spielman swallows and says You can't.

Yes you can.

They don't let canoes through the locks.

So? You can portage.

Spielman takes another bite, and Bobby's eyes go big. Jacob can be my partner!

For what?

Three-legged race, says Bobby. You can win this huge chocolate bar.

It's three pounds, says Cracker.

Yeah, says Dean, but who wants to drag your fat ass around?

Bobby shows Dean his chew and slips a shot to the shoulder. Cracks goes to nail him as well when he stops dead and Jacob sees the baldy-head shadow on the grass. They all turn and there he is, holding paper plates piled with sweating triangles and some chocolate on the side.

Hey there, boys.

Nobody says anything.

Want some? The Murph holds the plates out. Bobby reaches, but Cracks slaps his arm and says *No*, stupid.

I'm having some, says Dean. Looks the Murph right in the eye. Helps himself. One, two triangles, and a piece of chocolate.

That's more like it. Hungry man. Rest of you boys sure you don't want some? How 'bout you, Runner Boy? Too skinny. Need some meat on those –

The Murph's eyebrows bend like cats. He's looking back of Jacob. Jacob looks, too. Dad's still got a grin on. But not a nurse grin. What's goan on here?

Spielman bites the point off a triangle, shrugs.

Didn't ask you. I'm askin you. Dad jabs his finger at the Murph.

I'm just –

Piss off. I said *piss* off.

The Murph looks at Dad a bit, lets a breath out and heads off. Like a dog. A few people are looking on and whispering, but here's the director in his goofy chef's hat, asking if everything's all right here, and handing out little chocolate bars. Dad takes one and says Well thank you very much, your lordship. The director tries to smile it off but Dad says We'd all be better without the likes of *that* working for you, and he nods in the Murph's direction. The director huffs and mumbles like Joe Clark, and Dad – *Ach* – waves him off. Eyes Jacob and says See you, ten minutes.

But Bobby begs, and his mum says Let me have a word with your father, Jacob. Comes back and says It's okay, ties Bobby and Jacob together. Laughs when she has a look at them. I wish I had my camera – the two of you are like Laurel and Hardy.

Bobby holds his pudgy arm up and says Batman and Robin. Spielman, tied to Cracks, says More like Fatman and Beanpole. Bobby blows a raspberry at him and Dean says You're dead, but everyone's lining up.

Jacob says This way, Bobby. No, middle leg first. Don't even look at them. Look at the finish line.

Bobby nods. His face is red already.

You gonna be okay?

Bobby nods and says he hasn't had an attack since spring.

Good, 'cause we're gonna go fast. See your leg? No, the one tied to mine. Just pretend it's hollow. *I'll* move it, 'kay?

'Kay.

But you have to really *push* with the other one, got it? Try. Stea-*dy*, stea-*dy*. Good! But keep breathing.

'Kay.

And don't spaz out.

Nope, holy shit! Bobby points.

Jacob looks. The director's holding up the giant chocolate bar, and everyone watching claps. There's Dad. He winks. Jacob winks back, looks left and right down the line. Bulldog Quinn's way down the one end, tied to a Bastard. Other than them, Cracks and the Deaner are the main competition.

The director pulls a red flag from his back pocket. Holds it up. Ready?

Jacob and Bobby get their arms round each other.

And the director *swoosh* yells Go!

Bobby's face is all fat cheeks and fish lips, and Jacob can't look or he'll fall down laughing. Just keeps his eyes on the line and says

Stea-*dy*, stea-*dy*, and *swings* their leg *swings* their leg. Breathe, Bobby! Straight ahead! Stea-*dy*, *watch* the line watch the *line*! Jacob knows who Bobby's looking for. He can hear them. Yelling at each other –

Togetha, sucka –

– and falling.

Swing the leg.

We're winning, Jacob!

Behind him Jacob hears Dad laughing like never since the pahties. And he heaves Bobby through the string, falls on top of him and knucklerubs his head. Everybody cheers and claps – except the Murph, who's going round with a bag, picking up garbage, and Cracks and Dean, walking with their legs still tied together and arguing about whose fault it was.

Bobby holds up the chocolate bar like Moses, and Jacob gets to shake the director's hand. His teeth are probably all real, but his smile seems all fake.

At home after supper Dad says I suppose it was askin too much for Himself down there to give you one each?

Half's still pretty huge, Dad.

Suppose it is. Dad dunks a chunk in his tea, lets it soften up and drip. Still isn't used to chewing with his new teeth. They stick out like a horse's whenever he takes a bite. Jacob waits for him to wash it down before he says You sure showed that Murph guy.

Dads' face goes like it all – Piss off – just happened again, and he says See you, go near that guy and I'll thump you, hear me?

Jacob nods, swallows.

Bastard's lucky he didn't get a thumping as well.

He's pretty big, Dad.

Big. I took bigger guys than him in the army.

Greek guys?

Eh? No, Americans. Bigshot Marines over for training. Come into our canteens with their big fucken mouths – Dad puts on an American accent – Hey, *man*, wawt's with the skurt? Say that again? I says. Ah *sayd*, wawt's – *Bang* that's when I gave it them, right in the snoot. Dad taps his head. Glaswegian kiss, kid.

You hit them in the face with your head?

Do it right and you'll spread a guy's nose like jam.

Jacob swallows hard and says I think he was just taking watermelon round.

Hey, he shouldn't even fucken *be* there.

Maybe the director's just giving him a chance.

Doesn't need one. Have you any idea the money that bampot's got?

The Murph?

Aye, fucking Murphy. Owned his own business and all.

When?

'Fore his wife duffed herself. Sold the lot. Heavy machinery, it was. Had land up Hastings way as well. Sold that, too. Guy's got to have thousands stashed. Why he works in that friggin factory's a mystery to me.

You think, you think it's true, what people say about him?

Don't know, don't care, as long as he keeps to himself.

That's the first time I saw him except in his car.

Eh?

Downtown, I mean.

He say anything to you?

No.

Fuckingwell hope not, for his sake. That guy comes near you I'll split his skull for him. Now finish your chocolate and get at those dishes.

You going out?

Yeah.

Where to?

Mind your business.

Jacob lies awake that night, knocks his fists together as he imagines those big black and tan dogs – Get 'im, boys – hauling Dad down while the Murph watches. But at ten past one Dad comes in singing Pavarotti except quiet and all in his own funny words. Switches to whistling while he fries up the bits of fish they didn't eat at supper. He likes them on bread with a little cayenne pepper.

When I was a lad your age I used to go down the docks nearly every day.

Fishing?

Nope, stealin boats.

You stole boats?

Just wee ones mostly. Rowboats.

Did you ever get caught?

All the time.

Why did you steal them?

Was goan to Norway.

Jacob – Holy *jumpin* – smacks his head. Norway?

Yepsir. And I'd have done it, too. Packed my rations and all.

Why Norway?

Dad shrugs. Dunno, he says. Just wanted to see it. Vikings and all that.

But you got caught.

Dragged home by the bloody ear, and a hiding from your nana as well. Made it out pretty far once, though. Fisherman saw me. Radioed in. Good thing, too, size of the storm was brewin.

Maybe you would have made it, Dad.

You kiddin? We're talkin the North Sea, son. Vast.

I'd like to go to Norway, says Jacob, but Dad doesn't hear. He's staring down the river like it goes all the way to Oslo.

Tell us another one, Dad.

I've no recollection of this, but one day your Uncle Patrick bless his soul took me out in the pram. Let it go when a bug flew in his eye. It was a steep hill and – Dad cocks his head – hear that?

What?

Listen.

Jacob smiles and thinks of mermaids. But then he hears the echoes. It's Bobby, Dad.

Molly's boy?

Yeah.

What's he goan on about?

Jacob paddles harder. Dad, too. They round the bend just in time to see Cracker and Spielman up on the bluff. They've got hold of Bobby by his wrists and ankles. Swinging him out over the edge.

No! Let me go! Stop!

They toss him. But an ankle flops like a fish out of Spielman's hand, and Jacob hears the *crack* half a second after Bobby's head bounces off an outcrop. He hits the water limp.

Dad digs in his paddle and says Let's go, kid!

Bobby pops up flailing. Cracker dives in. Dean sees Jacob and Dad coming. And takes off.

Stroke, says Dad, *stroke*.

And Jacob goes hard. Keeps her straight.

Cracker swims crazy over to Bobby and tries to grab him but he's flailing too much, gets a mouthful, coughs and gags and flails some more.

Dad yells at Cracker. Away from him, son, away from him! Jacob – knees against the sides! That's it, steady now.

Bobby goes under.

Cracker screams Help.

And Dad doffs his life jacket. Looks back at Jacob. Can you get her into shore, son?

Jacob nods.

Your dad needs you now.

I know.

Right. Then *sploosh*, Dad breaks the water like an eel.

And Jacob starts paddling either side. Has a look.

Dad surfaces with his arms under Bobby's, hands either side of his head. Starts kicking his way to shore, stops and breathes in Bobby's mouth, keeps kicking.

Jacob hits shallow water, jumps from the canoe and hauls it in. Doffs his life jacket. Tears off his T-shirt. Rips it down the seam.

Cracker wades hard through the shallows, and says His head's wide open, over and over.

Here comes Dad now, Bobby in his arms. Now then, Graham, isn't it?

Cracker nods.

Listen to me, son. Get down to the park office, quick as you can. Tell them where we are and that we need an ambulance. Clear?

Cracker nods.

On you go, then.

Cracker climbs the bluff like the Black Panther. And Dad lays Bobby down. Palpates his head and neck and chest.

Oh God, Dad, look at the blood.

Calm down, son, calm down. It's no that bad. He looks back at Bobby, says Okay, nothing broken. Pulse. *There* it is. Right, we're okay, Dad says, but Jacob sees him eyeing the blood. Holds out the torn T-shirt and says Bandage.

Good job, son, give us it.

Jacob hands it over.

And Dad wraps Bobby's head. The red dot becomes a spot and a blotch before he even finishes.

He needs mouth-to-mouth, Dad!

Have a look, son, he's breathing. Just took one hell of a whack is all. Bobby, son, do you hear me? C'mon, son, you're all right.

His eyes flutter and he coughs and gags and cries.

It's all right, son, we've got you.

Up top, Cracker drops his bike near the edge and hollers It's coming, it's coming!

That was fast, lad, Dad says, well done.

But Cracker shakes his head. Spielman, he says between big breaths, he got there first and phoned. Ran all the way!

Jacob rides in the back of the ambulance with Graham and Dad, but he just remembers bits. The fracture board. The oxygen tank. Bloody bandage.

Dr. Smythe tells Dad he did a su-*peu*-lative job, but Dad just says Ach. Turns out Bobby's head wound is superficial. Sixteen stitches, but superficial. In overnight for observation, but Doc doubts there'll be any problems.

Outside X-ray, Molly Hollingsworth says Thank *God* you were there, John.

Nae bother, love. His nibs here could have done it by himself. Blindfolded. Eh, son? Dad slaps Jacob's shoulder.

But Jacob can't look at Mrs. Hollingsworth. Could maybe have wrapped Bobby's head right, but everyone knows Jacob can't swim for toffee. So his head whiplashes when he looks up and – smack – Mrs. H kisses him right on the mouth.

Bless you, too, she says, then looks back at Dad and tells him that when she sees that damn Spielman she'll break every bone –

Now now, Molly. It was an accident.

Accident my arse.

It was an accident, I'm telling you. We saw it. They were just being boys, Molly. Just boys being boys. Could have happened to any of them. Right, kid?

Mrs. H looks at Jacob, and he says Dad's right, Mrs. Hollingsworth. It was just an accident.

Bobby's hair looks like a cornfield in fall, but he's so happy, his scar hurts. All these comics, Jacob?

Sure.

You don't wanna trade or anything?

No.

Even *The Fantastic Fours?*

Jacob breathes out, but says Keep 'em.

Lucky *suck,* says Graham, and he whaps Bobby on the shoulder.

Bobby makes a face and shoves his scar at him. But in comes Mrs. Hollingsworth with a tray of grilled cheese sandwiches and tall glasses of milk.

Wow, thanks, Mrs. Hollingsworth.

You got it, hon. Hey, the two of you, that's enough.

Bobby grabs a sandwich and bites half in one go, says Thanks, Mom, around the mouthful.

Pig, says Cracker.

Bobby shows him his chew. Mrs. H just rolls her eyes and leaves.

And Jacob just chews and watches them carry on. Comes over every day while Bobby's stitches are still in, and every single time Mrs. Hollingsworth makes something good. Jell-O. Freshie. Sloppy joes. But the day that the stitches come out, Bobby and Graham's dad comes home from work early and says Get outside, Pete's sake. Shoves a new Nerf ball at Bobby and says Here, this hits you in the head it won't hurt.

Because of Neily Waldengarden Jacob can toss a pretty tight spiral and there's enough room in the Hollingsworths' yard to run plays, but Cracker and Bobby are not balletic receivers.

Cracker, I said left.

Yeah, Graham, he said left!

Shut up, scarhead. Sorry, Jacob.

Can I play?

Jacob turns. It's Spielman.

Yo ... honky, says Cracker. But he looks at Bobby.

Bobby kicks the ball back to Jacob and says I don't care.

Dean dumps his bike, steps on to the yard like it's ice and he's not wearing skates. McKnight, he says, and holds up his hands.

Jacob fades back, lets her fly. A little high.

Dean jumps and hauls it in.

Nice one, says Cracker, and it's like everybody, even the yard and the trees, sighs.

Bobby's hair grows like a weed, and Mrs. H treats Spielman like she's America and he's Russia. It's not long, though, before Spielman acts the hardman again. Not quite as much, maybe. When Jacob says No, he doesn't want to go hunting anymore, Spielman doesn't say anything with his mouth, just with his eyes. But sooner or later Dean'll shoot his mouth off and Jacob will have to face him – or just put up with him for one more Halloween, one more Christmas, one more Field Day, one more summer. Then it's high school, and Spielman will probably go into Level Four and do what all the other Fish and Chippers in Glanisberg do – take shop, bomb around in hot rods, fight and drink mickeys. For now they all have pretty good fun biking out to the quarry and playing ball, but it's too late. Everything's starting to change again. It's getting dark by eight, and, even with all the rain July had, a few of the leaves are dying already.

FOUR

This year, at least, it's down to Stedman's with Dad for the Back to School specials instead of second-hand stuff at the smelly Sally Ann. Jeans, two pairs, plus a shiny white windbreaker with red piping down the sleeves. Jacob lets on it's all the bee's knees, but new duds don't mean much when he thinks about Alvy. When he's walking across the parking lot first day back, pretending to read *A Handful of Dust* but looking for the white-blond hair, Jacob thinks So what if he doesn't come back. You're in Grade Eight now. Top of the school. Have to act like you don't give a rat's ass. Look at Spielman and Cracker. Leaning against the monkey bars, one foot up, thumbs in their belts. Girls walk by like nervous models and – is that Gail *McBride*? – giggle or say hi. It *is* Gail McBride, but she's got on gobs of makeup and a tight T-shirt – Styx, The Grand Illusion. Cracker elbows Spielman and nods at her ass, but Spielman makes like it's no big thing. Then he sees Jacob. Nods. Jacob nods. Lets on he's just hanging round, no bother. But he's shaking a little. Wanders all over the playground, looking, looking. Waits until way past last bell, and Mrs. Bunko, standing by the doors, says Jacob, do you want to spend your first morning with Mr. McCluskey?

No.

Then get in here.

Jacob looks where he thinks west is – how does Deaner just know north? – and says See ya, Alvy.

Jacob *McKnight*.

Sorry, he says, and jogs over.

Where's your homeroom?

Jacob shrugs.

Will you ever grow up?

Mrs. Bunko looks it up. Mr. Kazinski. Lucky. But even though Mr. K puts on Supertramp during geography – *Give* a little bit, give a little bit of your *love* to me! – the whole day feels like a math lesson Jacob doesn't get, makes him feel like decay inside.

Dad cuts into his hot turkey and wants to know how the big day went, like.

Didn't learn enough, Dad. Have to go back tomorrow.

And maybe even the day after that.

Never know.

See that what's-his-face with the moustache –

Kazinski –

Aye, him, see he keeps his opinions on training to himself this year. I'm still your coach.

Jacob nods, stares at gravy smears.

I imagine the girls liked your big-shot duds, says Dad.

Jacob shrugs.

Just wonderin, says Dad around a mouthful of spuds. Imagine you've got your eyes on a few by now?

Jacob's face goes hot and prickly, and he thinks Dad knows – I hear you in there at night, giving your pecker a pull – but he just keeps eating, and that night Jacob tries not to think of Gail. Her makeup was like *Hustler*, but her boobs – oh Gail, you are so lovely. Jacob imagines that his seminal vesicles are fully active and pumping the milk of creation way under her Mound of Venus. And he keeps going right till his pecker throbs like a heart, then he stops and pulls the sheet right over his head.

Son?

Yeah.

Up.

Coming.

Dad pushes it this morning, says *C'mon*, boy, let's *go*, when they hit the five-mile mark and Jacob starts to turn.

Just ten today, Dad.

We're doing twelve.

Dad, I can't.

Only another mile out.

And back.

So get a move on.

Jacob grits his teeth, picks it up. Passes.

Hey – medium pace.

But Jacob hits race pace. Burn in his chest. Good burn. By the time they get to the Murph's laneway again Dad can't say Watch out for dogs. He's winded.

And Jacob turns it on all the way into town. Lets it go down Bridge Street hill, and a couple of people on their way to work roll down their windows.

He's whuppin ya, Johnny!

But Jacob holds back, every stride whamming his knees, and lets Dad nose past at the last second. Most days Dad slows to a walk, hands on hips. Today he bends double. Gooby strings across his mouth. He breathes hard, looks at his watch. Jesus ... Christ ... kid, look at that: 1:21:02.

Could have broken 1:21, too, says Jacob.

I'll push you next time, says Dad.

The Cream of Wheat with honey goes down like a hot damn, but by the time Jacob gets to school, his knees and quads ache. Shouldn't have held himself back on that hill. Didn't drink enough fluids either. Headache. So Jacob blinks and thinks it's a mirage by the monkey bars. Blinks again. It isn't. It's him.

Alvy?

He doesn't hear.

Alvy! Hey, Alvy!

His knees groan, but Jacob breaks into a sprint. Yells Alvy's name again. Still he doesn't hear. Or just doesn't turn around. Jacob slows, walks, stops. Holy jumpin. It's him all right, but what'd he do to his hair?

Al-vy?

He turns.

And Jacob's eyes bug out. Get The Knack, says Alvy's shirt, and he's wearing an earring.

Al-vy?

Hey, McKnight, how's it going?

Jacob tries to look past the getup, but over Alvy's shoulder he sees her instead – Gail.

Hi, Jacob.

Oh. Hi. Sorry.

Alvy shrugs like he's a big rebel or something. Could be smoking a cig the way he's standing there, that look on his face. And it's just a little gold ball, but Jacob can't keep his eyes off the earring. Only a few guys in Glanisberg have earrings, and most of them are Chippers who listen to Black Sabbath, or disco guys who get beat up by Chippers. Dad says *any* guy with an earring is a poofta. The left ear means you pitch, the right means you catch. That's how it was in the British Navy, which, says Dad, was full of English pooftas. Alvy's is in the left, but he's putting the playboy moves on. Pinches Jacob's sleeve like it's money and says Cool jacket.

Thanks. When did you get back?

Like he's Neily Waldengarden just in from Paris, Alvy says My flight landed yesterday. Don't really need to be here on the first day, anyway, you know?

Sure. So, how was your brother's?

Totally cool, says Alvy.

What'd you do?

Alvy tosses his bangs. This and that, he says and sniffs. I went to Vancouver with my bro, hung with some friends he has there, you know.

Jacob can't picture Vancouver except for totem poles and very big trees, but the way Alvy says Vancouver, it sounds like the place where you Get The Knack and your ear pierced. So Jacob says Cool, even though he knows it sounds fake, faker than Alvy. What he wants to say is What *happened*? or It's great you came back, but the words stop behind his teeth and all he can manage is What home-room y'in?

Richardson again.

Oh. I'm Kazinski. Sit beside you in art though.

Alvy's nod says Sure, maybe, but then he props himself against the monkey bars, his hand right near Gail's head, and his eyes say *Later*.

And Jacob eyes the scar. Could give it a crack. But he says Guess I'll see you, and before he can say *at lunch* or *after school* or even *this weekend*, Alvy says A-*round*, man.

Jacob runs across the playground to where Spielman and the guys are playing foot hockey with a tennis ball. Cracker kicks it out of bounds. Jacob snags it, points at Cracker, and says I'm on your team. Tosses the ball in play. Spielman traps it and says McKnight talks to faggots.

Spielman, says Cracks, shut yo jive-ass mouth and let da man play.

Hollingsworth, says Spielman, get new lingo. Then he kicks the ball to Bulldog and says Game on.

And Jacob plays like no tomorrow. Hip-checks Bobby – Hey, McKnight, come off it! – but gets bounced bad by Spielman when he takes his eyes off the ball and sees Alvy and Gail heading behind the portable.

You clotheslined me, asshole.

Keep your head up, asshole.

Miss Richardson sees the whole thing, walks over. What's going on here? Jacob?

Nothing, he says.

So what's with all the roughhousing?

You should check behind the portable, Miss R. I think people are making out back there.

Really. Anything else, sir?

No, says Jacob, and he turns and winks at Cracker, nothing else.

Why the act? says Miss Richardson, but Jacob pretends not to hear. Tosses the ball at Spielman's chest and says Next goal wins.

In art class, Alvy sits in the opposite corner. Stares a lot – out the window, at Gail. Mrs. Bunko moved her up front, but she twirls hair around her finger, draws hearts on her pencil case.

A.C.
+
G.M.

What a joke. At least when Spielman gets a girl he's not connected at the waist. Alvy is. Walks her to school. Walks her home. Gimpy One and Gimpy Two. Science partners. Sit there on the swings and stare at each other like paintings. Except when they neck.

Jacob turns over his perspective, starts a sketch of Arsenal and X-Calibre. Blasting through a wall. Wants to show Alvy, but he barely looks in this direction. And here comes big Bunko, her eyebrows bent like question marks.

Finished, Jacob says, and he shows her his drawing.

An orchard?

Yeah.

What's that, under the tree?

Dead bird.

I've seen you do better, Mrs. Bunko says, but what she really means is Good, but sit and do something quiet. She keeps walking up the aisle, looking over shoulders. Jacob digs Evelyn Waugh out of his Adidas bag, but checks his shoulder one more time. Alvy's looking toward the front of the class and back down at his paper, front of the class, paper. Pencil going like mad. Jacob follows the sightline. To Gail. Alvy's drawing Gail.

Jacob opens the Waugh but can't read a line right now. Says to himself I can disappear, too, Mr. Knack. You'll see.

Outside, the wind blows like down Sterling Road, and a maple tree leans way over. The yellow leaf near the top can't hold on and falls, spins, falls. Soon art'll be paper pumpkins and witches. Monster drawings. Masks.

Jacob pretends *A Handful of Dust* is like a bible, prays for the clock to stop. To go backwards. All the way to June, and the orchard, but this time he'd see that blue jay before Spielman and yell at it to fly.

But the clocks only ever go back an hour, and Spielman starts assigning stores on a rotating basis. You have to buy milk or something, too, so no one gets suspicious. Then they bury them, the eggs, back of Spielman's Garden Centre. Bobby asks Jacob if he's really coming out this year. Jacob says he will.

But he said that last year.

And the year before, too.

The year before that, Jacob was the Flash.

And Cailan was Green Lantern, the Flash's best friend.

Dad painted the big green ring. And Mum made both their costumes. Started sewing in September. So Jacob starts his drawings now, even though her birthday's not till November 17. He wants to draw her, but he can't see her face. Her real face, not the face he remembers after the accident, before she left. When she threw the ashtray, or just wouldn't get out of bed. Puffy. Eyes like shiners almost. Or like the women Picasso painted – all teeth and angles and mad bulging eyes. Jacob can see it, her real face, for a heartbeat sometimes, but one blink later and it's a blur. So the night before Halloween, Dad away at work, Jacob stands before the closed closet door, swallows hard and opens it. Pushes Dad's clean uniforms to either side and hauls out the boxes he never unpacks. On top in the biggest is a jumble of Dad's old ties. Jacob untangles the shiny silver one he remembers from the wedding pictures, but doesn't know how to tie a proper knot. Just drapes it round his neck. Opens the black leather case. Slides the gold ring on his thumb. Holds cufflinks up to the light. Shiny black ones and dark blue ones, and ruby red ones, and tiger eyes. Then he lifts the ties out, and touches, just touches, Dad's musty tunic, the Black Watch kilt. The hairy sporran. The long wool socks. And the wee skean-dhu. Jacob slides it out the sheath, breathes *hwah,*

hwah on both sides of the blade, shines it on his shirt. Turns it this way, that, to see his own face. Puts it back in the sheath, slides it down his sock. The rest he leaves where it is because Dad folded it all so careful.

He always says It was your Mum got the lot, the *lot*. But she left behind the photos. Two albums, plus the wedding pictures and piles of Polaroids in envelopes from the hospital. First hair-cuts – Cailan's crying. Third birthdays, both of them blowing out a 3-shaped candle either end of the white cake with their names crossed in bright bright red.

JACOB
A
I
L
A
N

He dumps out another envelope. Second-grade school pictures, Jacob lost his front teeth first. The pirate boat, and Cailan with the cutlass. Dad in the water, waving. Mum like a pin-up on the bow of a speedboat. Mum posing on the Parisienne's hood. Mum at the beach in a blue bikini. Dad at the beach, making his bicep look bigger. Mum in a parka, piles of snow behind her, push-ing a stroller with Cailan or Jacob, it's impossible to tell, their snowsuits were the same.

Another envelope. Lots of these ones are getting old and faded. From way before they were born, even, when it was just Mum and Dad up at the mines in Renabi. And even though Jacob can see her face a hundred times if he wants – Mum pumping a cuff to check a miner's BP, Mum by a wall chart teaching basic first aid – Jacob wonders how he could ever draw her voice, 'cause that's what he hears right now, Mum's voice, bits of all her stories about life in the bush and mine camps. Gettin off that train near Renabi north of nowhere, let me tell you, I wondered what on *earth* have I done? But this was it, this was Canada, and we soldiered on, your father and I. And wouldn't you know it was wundaful. Go back in a second, I would. How come, Mummy, yeah, how come? Hawd life, but the characters you meet, good

Lord. Like who like who? Well, your father, for one. A wild man he was, his beard to here – He had a *beard*? – Yes, he did, and singin and dancin on tables, but he cared about those men, let me tell you. Risked his own life to get them out if there was an accident. Working night and day for that little house. Where the moose was? Yes, that's right, bears in your trash and one morning a moose, up to here, good Lord. I wrote your nanna and she said what's a moose, think of a great big horse with antlers, I told her. I remember the moose! Me, too! No now now, you were both too little. Barely see the two of you sometimes all bundled up against the cold. Just two little noses between the hood and the scarf. Lord love a duck I never knew cold like that, and this Frenchie would look at the two of you, O what was his name now, and say Dare da same dare da same! Always getting injured, he was, and your dad bringing him in. Trompin through the snow to the railway tracks in the dark with me little lamp, wavin it so the train knew to stop. Those were the days to test your mettle. I do so remember the moose, Mum. Jakey's a good rememberer, Mum. So he is, my little duck egg, so he is.

Cross-legged, with all the photos spilled around him, and his elbows on his calves, Jacob presses his palms hard against his eyes. Stays like that, wondering where to begin. Stays like that till his bum and back are aching and the skean-dhu has made dents in his skin. All these bits and pieces around him, a hundred of her faces, but now that he's seen them, he thinks that a drawing of her would look dead as doornail compared.

And why does she have to have a boyfriend, anyway. Or maybe even – *No*, says Jacob – a second husband. No – he looks and looks through the photos, dumps out every envelope and spreads photos all over the floor. Can't find it, but he *remembers* it, he remembers it, the one where they got Best Couple. It looks like Dad has real armour. And a long white robe, rosy cross on the chest and another one going down the nose of his helmet, and you couldn't even tell it was a Kentucky Fried bucket he painted it so real. And his broadsword was perfect, too, except he cut his thumb carving it, and Mum kept pricking herself sewing her sky-blue robes and the

train hanging off her tall pointy hat. They won a trophy that someone made and everything. Best Couple. But Jacob can't find it.
Wipes snot on his wrists and gathers everything up. Puts it all back
just the way he found it.

After school the next day, Jacob just lies there on the chesterfield, thinking about all the costumes kids wore to school. Lot of witches and ghosts, gee, that's original, but there were some good ones. Danny St. Jacques was c-3po with real metal bits and everything, and went around all day going Oh my, we *are* in a fix. Hardly anyone else in Grade Eight dressed up, but Alvy and Gail came as the Fonz and Pinky Tuscadero. The leather jacket used to be his brother's. Dean said only dickheads watch *Happy Days*. But at least they have costumes. Cracks said he'd steal a pair of his mom's pantyhose, and Jacob could just be a robber. He doesn't want to be a robber. He doesn't want to be anything. Or do anything. Just lie here. Except it's time to get the supper on. And be okay for Dad. Not much in the fridge, though. He gets pretty forgetful this time of year. Jacob puts on a pot of water, holds the jar of Ragu under the tap – *one* one thousand – and gives it a good shake. The Gran Torino pulls in just when the sauce starts to simmer. Jacob just keeps stirring when Dad comes in.

Spaghetti tonight, is it?

Jacob turns. Holy jumpin!

Dad's got a case of Tahiti Treat under one arm, a six-pack of Golden under the other and a fat grocery bag hanging from his right wrist. Payday, boyo. Use a new jar.

You bet!

Dad whumps the cases on the counter. Get these in the fridge, will you, son?

Sure.

I'll get out my togs, then we'll sit down for a good wee nosh. Sound all right?

You bet. What's in the bag?

This? Just some candy, like. In case we get any kids.

Jacob tries not to squint. They never get kids.

Dad turns around, reaches in the bag, turns back and says Oh, there's this, too. And slaps *whap, whap* a tin of custard powder plus a four-pack of jelly rolls on the counter. Jacob says That's the *best*, and Dad has a laugh. Stuffs the plastic bag – still pretty full – up under his arm, tells Jacob he'll be right back. Sings Neil Diamond – Sep-tember morn – in the bedroom while he's changing. By the time he comes out, the spaghetti's ready.

Looks good, kid. Wantin a pop?

You bet.

Dad gets a Tahiti Treat and a Golden, opens them both, and – There you go, boyo – has a seat. Cheers!

Cheers, Dad.

Tunk. And they both take a good long haul.

Between his fork and spoon Dad lifts spaghetti up to eye level, makes sure everything's evenly coated. Jacob just twirls with his fork. Chews, and waits.

So then. How was school?

Didn't learn enough. Have to go back tomorrow.

Nothin special then?

Nope. Just costume parades. For the kids.

Dad stares at his spaghetti for a few seconds, and Jacob wonders if they're going to talk about tomorrow and the flowers and all now. But Dad just takes a haul. Shivers. Says the beer's good and cold. Spins and spins spaghetti in his spoon. Jacob hunches because of the scraping sound. Eats as much as he can, but Dad can't finish his, either.

Sorry, Dad, always make too much.

Left some room, I hope.

Little, says Jacob, and he gets up, clears the table.

Dad sucks back the last of his beer. Well then, guess I'd better get that custard on. Jacob nods, has everything washed, the empties put away and the kettle on as the custard starts to suck and pop. Dad makes it with no lumps ever, and he layers it over the jelly rolls like art. There y'are, kid.

Thanks.

Jacob's scraping custard off the sides of his bowl when Dad says So. You never said nothin 'bout what you want to be this year.

Jacob licks his spoon, swallows. Not going to be anything this year.

Why's that?

I'm twelve now, Dad.

Oh, aye, ancient. What about the lads then?

Jacob shrugs. They're all going, he says.

What will the Hollingsworth boys be this year, I wonder?

Who cares.

Eh, fine, suit yourself. Guess you'll no be needin the costume I got you.

You got me a costume?

Dad shrugs.

What is it?

Interested all of a sudden?

Jacob nods.

Right, says Dad. Stand there, and keep your eyes closed.

Jacob walks then jumps to where Dad pointed. Cracks an eye when Dad comes back from the bedroom with the grocery bag. No peekin.

What is it, Dad?

You'll see.

Jacob hears plastic torn open, and something clinks when it hits the linoleum.

Yepsir, you wait and see what your old Dad's done. So simple. Can't believe I didn't think of this before.

Pressure on Jacob's leg. He peeks.

Bandages. Rolls and rolls of them. And a bag of metal clips. Dad's wrapping, wrapping wrapping up the leg. Right, son, have a look.

Jacob tries to look like it's Christmas.

And Dad says What do ya think of *that*, eh? Totally realistic!

I'm the Mummy?

Who else wears bloody bandages?

Just the Mummy.

'Zactly. Now, stand still.

His head by Jacob's belly, Dad passes the roll from one hand to the other. This'll be great, son, this'll be great. His knees crack as he stands and wraps Jacob's chest, then he loops the roll under Jacob's left armpit. Clips it. Wraps the arm, layer, by layer, by layer, clips the bandage just above the wrist. You'll be needing your hands, I'm sure.

Jacob can't talk. Just nods.

And Dad does the right arm, loops the armpit. Clips. Gets another roll and starts the neck.

Not too tight, is it, son?

Jacob shakes his head as much as he can.

And Dad clips behind the neck, gets another roll. Now, he says, pinning the gauze to Jacob's chin with his thumb, the pièce de résistance. I'm telling you, boyo, you'll be the envy of everyone. Better than what's-his-name, Karloff, *The Mummy*.

Jacob remembers the movie when Dad wraps his head. The young pharaoh. Captured. Tongue torn out with tongs.

Breathe, kid, you're not underwater.

The breath, *phooh*, hits him back in the face.

Good. Now just close your eyes a minute.

Ca' *see*.

Just hang on a minute. Dad wraps, wraps, wraps.

Da.

Almost done.

Da, ca' breave.

Just one second, 'sakes. Dad adds another clip back of Jacob's left ear. Walks away.

Da!

I'm right here.

Jacob hears the snap of a button, and metal against leather, and the *snik snak* of Dad's special ambulance scissors. Can cut through a penny.

Hold still, kid.

Jacob freezes.

You hear me?

Nod.

Right then. We'll fix you right up.

The crunch of cut gauze, the cold edge against Jacob's lips. Then *air*.

There now. How's that?

Phooh.

Good, says Dad, now keep your eyes *shut.*

Dad, don't.

Just hold still now, your old dad knows what he's doing.

Snip, snip, snip. And there's Dad's face. Bingo, he says, you're ready, kid.

Jacob takes a stiff step backwards, nearly falls. Dad, I can barely move.

Bit too tight, is it? Hang on a minute.

Snik snak, snik snak and Dad says S'poze the Mummy should look a wee bit tattered.

Flaps of bandage hanging off him, Jacob takes a big step, two.

Hang on, son. Just thought of something. A last wee touch, like.

Jacob stands, blinks, breathes.

Behind him, Dad opens the oven door. Jacob peg-legs around, sees Dad on his knees, his arms way in the oven, rubbing his hands on the bottom. He slides them out, holds them up. They look scorched. Good thing that hasn't been cleaned, he says.

Jacob backs up.

Where you goan? This is exactly what you're needin.

And Dad smears Jacob head to toe. Stands back and says Fucken magic! Lifts his arms in front of him, moans and drags his left leg. He stops, spits in his hands, smacks them. Your old Dad's an artist! he says, and nods at the bathroom. Go on and have a look!

And Jacob's eyes bulge against the bandage edges when he sees himself, but his belly aches. For Dad, and how he tries. Payday, boyo, use the new jar. Jelly rolls and stolen bandages.

C'mon out here, kid, and let's have another look at you.

Jacob gimps out of the bathroom. Great costume, Dad.

Wonder where that old camera is. Wait till I have a look.

Dad.

Eh?

Just thought of something.

What?

What if I need to go?

Go where?

Jacob points at his crotch.

Oh. See what you mean. Eh, suppose you'll just have to tie a knot in it.

Dad.

I know what I can do. Hang on a tic.

Dad gets his scissors. *Snik snak*. Hold still, he says, till I cut it off. Easy, 'sakes, I'm just kidding. C'mere. Dad cuts a hole. Then clips the piece back on and says There, emergency door. If you need it.

Hope not.

Now, says Dad, where did I put that old camera?

Should get going, really.

Oh.

The guys. They always meet at Spielman's. Six-thirty.

Oh. On you go then.

In his bedroom, Jacob yanks the pillow from its case. Stutter-steps to the door, gets his shoes on.

Dad looks him up and down and laughs. Marathon Mummy, he says.

Jacob looks down. Shrugs. Gotta go, Dad.

Hey.

Jacob penguins round.

Yeah?

I haven't forgotten, you know.

I know.

Could you talk to Judy Spielman about the flowers while you're there?

I think she just knows to do it now.

We'll go tomorrow as usual then?

Jacob nods.

So see you don't come home in a cop car, says Dad.

Jacob freezes, but Dad smiles when he says Bill Philips down Becker's tells me you lot developed a sudden fondness for eggs a while back.

Jacob waits.

But Dad smiles again. On you go, dafty. I'll tell you a few Guy Fawkes stories sometime. But see you don't get intae any serious shit now, hear me?

Jacob nods. V-legs down the patio steps. And Dad's laugh disappears behind the gently closed door.

Jacob plants his right foot like a compass point, heaves himself around the corner to Oliver Street and huff puffs – Like an oven in here – up to Spielman's. The wrapping around his legs and waist – Dad have to do so many *layers*? – loosens a little, but Jacob still has to stutter step, and that must increase, he figures, his Mumminess because he scares the crap out of a group of little kids all dressed up like Peter Pan people. Captain Hook flips up his patch and both his eyes bulge and he says Get out of the way, to Tinkerbell and the Crocodile, who doesn't see Jacob until the last second because his head and snout are so big. Peter Pan waves his little sword and says I'll kill it, but Jacob says Can't, you little shit, Mummy's already dead. Then he goes boo-*waa*, and they all scream and run away.

Everybody waiting up at Spielman's hears the hubbub, and Bobby, Luke Skywalker except fat, points his lightsabre and says Hey, everyone, look at McKnight!

Dean's mum and Mrs. Hollingsworth laugh and clap their hands and Mrs. H says Heavens to Betsy. Cracks, who has the perfect head for it, looks just like Frankenstein with bolts in his neck and everything. Costume, he says, gooood. But Spielman, Dracula for the second year in a row, just says Didn't think you'd come.

Dean, says Mrs. Spielman. Don't listen to him, Jacob.

I was just getting my costume ready, Jacob says.

Mean your dad was? says Spielman.

I helped, so go suck an *egg*, Drac.

Try, says Mrs. Spielman, to get along, boys, for just one night? And no, she says, and knuckles Dean on the head, I mean *no* trouble.

You can see Spielman going red even under his white makeup, but he says Let's go already, we'll miss the candy apples.

Jacob walks quick as he can but still brings up the rear – with Bobby, who takes a haul on his puffer and says Wish *I* was the Mummy.

Your costume's great, Bobby.

Yours is better. Yours is the best.

Jacob could almost call it off right now except maybe for a couple of candy apples and the Trident mints that Dr. Helfgott gives out. Head home and hug Dad and say it was the best Halloween of all time. But if he does that, Spielman's voice will follow him halfway down the street and all around the schoolyard for two days. McKnight balked. McKnight ran. Chick-en. Right, thinks Jacob. Easy enough to chuck an egg until some Fish and Chipper like Garth Greer or Shawn Quinn has you by the hair. Pound the living snot out of you.

Jacob slows down, waves Bobby over.

What?

Screw this with the eggs stuff. Let's stay trick-or-treating.

Deaner'd kill us, Jacob.

Chippers'll kill us if we get caught.

I won't get caught. Climb a tree no sweat and stay up there if I have to.

Bobby, I can't run. Can barely *walk*.

You can just be the Mummy for candy and then you can take the bandages off.

Don't want to wreck it, says Jacob, but Bobby's already running over to Mrs. Norman's. She's at the door, bending over open bags and putting her homemade candy apples in. Mrs. Norman and Mrs. O'Toole just up the street make them every year, but only two or three trays. After that it's caramels and two-packs of Chiclets.

Mrs. Norman goes gaga over Jacob's costume, and so must Mrs. O'Toole because when the other guys have gotten theirs she sneaks two candy apples in Jacob's pillowcase. For you and your father, dear.

Shoulders square and chest out, Jacob tells himself he'll throw a few eggs, all right. No big whoop. And his bandages are loosening up, too. Can almost walk normal now.

They work their way up the street, but Spielman hurries. Except for Trick or treat or Wow, thanks for the Chiclets, he doesn't say anything until they all double back to the burial spot. Then he pulls a little flashlight out his pocket, shines it in Bobby's face, then at the shovel under the tree, and says Dig.

He doesn't have the air, says Jacob.

So, says Spielman, and he shines the light in Jacob's eyes, you dig. Hardly bought any eggs.

Cracker says *Me*, shovel. And digs a lot faster than he talks.

Cracker and Bobby take out the cartons and Spielman starts loading his pockets. Gives Jacob the once-over, shakes his head.

That ain't nothin, says Cracker, he can be our ammo man. None of us got enough pockets for all these anyway. Here, Jacob, gimme your pillowcase.

Maybe I should just go.

Just give it here.

Cracker shoves Jacob's candy to one side, puts two cartons of eggs in, covers them up as much as he can with candy from everybody's bags.

Back on the street Spielman says they'd better trick-or-treat a few more houses to look natural and all. Jacob thinks his pillowcase looks like a pillowcase with two cartons of eggs and some candy in it, so he just stays down by the sidewalk and says I've got lots, thanks, when people ask Doesn't the Mummy want some, too? About every other house Cracker or Bobby gives Jacob a little of what they got unless it's really good like mini Mars bars.

They go up Nasby and turn onto Margaret when – Holy *shit*, says Bobby – a Chipper's hot rod with one of those whatsits sticking out the hood cruises *glub-blub-blub* round the corner. Whoever's driving squeals the tires and swerves toward Jacob and the guys. Chippers lean out the window and hoot and holler. The woman still in the doorway of the last house yells Slow *down*, cement-heads, there are kids around. After she lets the screen door slam shut Spielman says Okay, enough candy – it's fun time.

Great, Jacob thinks.

Spielman points up Cromwell. Side street, not so many lights. They walk along like it's nobody's business, waiting for a car, eyeing houses, wondering who'll have the guts.

Spielman stops and turns and stares at Bobby.

Un-unh, no way, I'm first all the time no way.

Didn't say you, did I? says Spielman. McKnight.

What.

Chuck one.

An egg?

No. A candy apple.

Where?

Spielman shrugs.

Anywhere?

Sure.

That house right there.

It's dark. No one's home.

So. Get it right in the big window. Boosh.

Go ahead.

Watch me.

I'm watching.

Jacob reaches into his pillowcase, cracks a carton. Looks this way, that. Group of kids way down the other end of the street. No faces in windows. Okay. He fakes a wind-up, and even Spielman, along with everyone else, starts to scatter.

Yeah, look who's chicken now, says Jacob.

Just throw it, says Spielman.

Jacob tries. The egg lands *plik* in the house's front yard. Doesn't even break.

Everybody just stares at it for a second, then Spielman holds his head and says Holy *shit*, McKnight, that was totally fucking *useless*.

It's my bandages, arsewipe. I can't throw.

Go get it.

You go get it.

You threw it, *you* go get it.

Who lives here, anyway? says Bobby.

Who *cares?* says Spielman. *Get* it, McKnight.

Jesus okay fine, says Jacob. He has a look, tiptoes across the lawn. When he bends over one of his clips *pling* pops off and a bandage flaps and a light blinks on in the house's hallway and – *boof-boof* – two eggs hit the front door's window. Behind Jacob, Spielman laughs and Cracker says Run. And Bobby's yelling Wait! and the front door *booms* open and a man – You little *fucker* – comes for Jacob like a football player.

Jacob takes off, tears at bandages.

You are *dead*, you little shit!

Up ahead Spielman asshole and Cracker and Bobby bastards duck into backyards. Jacob tears away more bandages that Dad wrapped so careful Spielman you are fucking –

I said c'mere!

It wasn't even me! And Jacob rips bandages from his face, *air*, his crotch, *faster*, and –

Gotcha!

– his head lashes back and his legs leave the ground which *crack* he hits with the bag right under him.

The man heaves and huffs and looks at Jacob's face and says Get up.

It wasn't even me I swear!

Get up.

He gets hold of Jacob, and marches him back up the street, one hand like a vice around Jacob's neck, the other wrapped around his bicep. He squeezes so hard one of the clips bites right through the bandage and shirt sleeve into Jacob's arm.

Not so tight.

Shut up.

I didn't even throw –

Get up there, says the man, and he shoves Jacob up the pathway to the door.

My *wife*, the man says, has *pneumonia*. First time she could sleep never mind breathe in three days and *Jesus* look at the fucken mess.

I'm sorry she's sick but –

Shut your face and clean it.

Jacob tries a wipe with the bandages on his arm but just smears egg all over the window.

Light comes on in the hallway. Here comes the guy's wife. Blue housecoat, slippers, Windex bottle in one hand and a roll of paper towel in the other. The look of her. Like a zombie.

Jacob steps back when she opens the door.

Whoa, says the man. Honey, let *him* do that. You go back to –

She gives him a look, sprays the window and says Just take him home.

Ma'am, says Jacob, I'll do it.

Gary, says the woman, take him home.

Damn right I will, and I'll tell his parents just as soon –

No, says Jacob. I, I'll walk home. Just let me, I'll clean it all.

Let him do it, honey.

Please, ma'am.

The woman taps Jacob's breastbone with the Windex nozzle. Go ... home.

Big Gary swears under his breath and then says Let's go. Lucky I don't call the goddamn cops on you.

The cops, thinks Jacob, are nothing compared.

Dad looks like he just took a jab in the mug when he opens the door and sees the two of them there. But then he stands straight like a soldier and listens and nods when Big Gary tells him what went on and my *wife* is the one back there cleaning up the mess what kind of shit is *that*? Eh? He jabs his finger in Dad's face.

And Dad looks at the finger. Sets his lips. I'd be happy, he says, to clean all your windows. Professional job. Any time you like. Used to be my trade years ago.

Gary snorts and Jacob says But Dad I swear I –

See you, says Dad. Shut your mouth and *in*-side. He jerks his thumb over his shoulder.

Jacob goes in, steps out of his shoes. Dad's eyes on him as he turns and closes the door behind him, saying Now then, Gary, I appreciate you coming, let's you and me head down the stair, like, and –

Jacob just stands in the kitchen, waits. Hears Gary yelling something at the bottom of the stairs. Then nothing. Then a *thud*. And another.

Then Dad walks, whistling, up the stairs. Gary yells again and starts his Buick and revs too hard before peeling out.

Dad walks in. His face.

And Jacob looks at the tatters of his costume, and shakes.

Christ, boy, says Dad, look at the state of you. And he starts laughing.

Jacob's eyes widen, bulge, blink.

And Dad's still laughing and saying he wishes he had a camera Chrissake look at the *state* of you. He comes over and Jacob steps back, thinking he's for it anyway. But Dad's hand curls round Jacob's neck. He pulls him closer, and pats him, and Jacob leans into his chest and shoulder and says It was the best costume ever, Dad. Everyone said.

'Sall right. Who's that bampot think he is, anyway, coming round here and pointing his finger in my face.

Did you –

Never you mind what I did. What you'll do is go round with your pals and clean all his windows. Tomorrow.

Dad.

Eh what am I sayin. Day after.

The day after, sure.

Now get out of this mess, Christ, and jump in the bath. I'll get some tea on.

Next day it's Dean comes out the back of the shop with the arrangement and the wreath. After his mum gives him a look, he says I'm sorry, Jacob.

Jacob takes the wreath from him and says 'Bout what.

Dean glances at Dad, looks down and says Me and Cracker. We went by that guy's place, and told him who did it and all.

Mrs. Spielman gives Dad a grin and – I won't take no for an answer, John – a good deal on the flowers. Dad grins back and says They're beautiful.

A week later, Jacob walks back to Mount Pleasant after school. He's never gone alone before. It was the headstone, how it always seemed to whisper You did it. Now he can touch it. Eyes open. Feeling with his fingers the name, Cailan Patrick McKnight, and the Gaelic writing that Dad can speak like song. *Ar dheis Dé go raibh a anam.*

Jacob gives it a go – Are desh jay ge row a anam – and then, because Mum is, he says it in English. May his soul be on God's right side.

It's been awful windy this week, and Jacob has to straighten the arrangement, but, say what you want about Dean Spielman, his folks sell flowers that last.

At home, Jacob says Still looking good, Dad.

Eh?

The flowers.

You went up, did you?

Hope that's okay.

Course it is, son.

Should I get supper going?

Come on with me to Sharpe's first. We should do a proper shop.

I'll start the car.

Dad tosses the keys, says I'll just be two tics. Off he goes to the washroom. Likes to comb his hair before he goes out now, and even splash a little Mennen on.

Jacob turns the Torino over, slides across the front seat. Out comes Dad, whistling. Stops when he gets in and says Get your belt on.

Yep. Jacob asks Dad what he was whistling on the way up to Sharpe's.

I dunno. How did it go?

Jacob gives it a try, but just gets spit and air.

Like this, son. Dunnae force it, just let the sound come out, like.

That's the one you were just whistling.

Oh, aye, it's called 'Mull of Kintyre.'

Old Scottish song?

Old Scottish place, but it's a new song. That wee fruit from the Beatles did it.

Paul McCartney?

Aye, him.

He's not a fruit.

Suit yourself.

Thought you liked the Beatles.

I do, but half of they Wings songs are bloody awful. 'Mull of Kintyre' isnae bad, though. Pipes and all in it.

Where is it?

Mull of Kintyre? Argyll. Show you it someday.

We'll go to Scotland?

Time you knew your hisstree.

I like Robert the Bruce.

Well, I'll take you to Bannockburn as well then. Once we get out the hole your mother left us in, I should be able to set aside a few bucks.

Jacob just stares out the window for the rest of the drive.

Right then, how are we on bread?

'Bout half a loaf left.

Cereal?

Need it.

G'wan and get some then, and meet me over in Produce.

'Kay.

Jacob has a look at Lucky Charms and Frosted Flakes and Fruit Loops, thinks of asking, but tosses Cream of Wheat in the cart. Tries to whistle when he gives the cart a good push and, arms out, balances on the pushbar. Nearly crashes when he sees Alvy and his mum. Over by the Chinese vegetables. Takes a step back, but holy jumpin, look at Mrs. Chatwin. Hairstyle. Makeup. New coat.

She looks up.

And Jacob ducks behind the aisle. Keeps one eye on her and Alvy, another on Dad, and sneaks between the spuds and the turnips. Dad's looking at mushrooms. Pops a fat white one in his mouth.

Quietly, Jacob says Dad.

Eh? Oh. What'd you do, take a lap round the store?

Sorry. Guess we better get going.

What's your hurry?

Jacob shrugs, has a quick look. Alvy and his mum move along to spinach.

You'd think, says Dad, they'd have better mushrooms, price you pay. Though you could fry these up with some onions and a beef cutlet, and they'd be a bit of all right.

Cutlets, says Jacob, let's get some. And he starts heading to Meats – just when Mrs. Chatwin sees him. And her expression opens like fireworks. Maybe she doesn't even remember when Jacob came by the house. Or does remember, and wants to colour over it. Here she comes round the plums, wonky wheel on her cart g-dug-dug-dug against the floor. And Alvy behind her, the rest of his face crowded around the lie of his smile.

Well, hi there, Jacob!

Hi.

How are ya, dear? One eye keeps drifting in Dad's direction when Jacob says I'm fine, hey, Alvy.

Hey.

Mrs. Chatwin clears her throat. Alvy takes his hands out of his pockets, sticks out the right one. Hello, Mr. McKnight, I'm Alvy.

Hallo yourself, lad.

They shake, and Mrs. Chatwin says Well I knew it. I've seen you out and about and I just knew you must be Jacob's father. Such a resemblance.

Just as ugly as his old dad, I'm afraid.

Just as handsome. Alice. Alice Chatwin.

Eh, John McKnight. Pleased to meet you.

They shake.

Helluva grip, says Dad.

Old farm girl ... yeah, nice to meet you.

Jacob stares at a plum that's fallen from its pyramid and onto the floor. Alvy puts it back.

So, Alice, Dad says, new to the old town, you are.

Oh, not that new. Originally from this area.

That right, now?

Mm-hmm. Is that a Scottish accent?

'Deed et is.

I've always loved that accent, eh, Alv? I'm half Scotch, myself.

Scotch is a drink.

Sorry?

No mind. What's the other half?

English.

Won't hold it against ye, says Dad, grinning big.

Mrs. Chatwin laughs but it turns into a gravelly cough, and Alvy looks at cauliflower. Turns a twist tie around the end of his finger. Pardon me, says his mum, pat-pat-patting her chest.

Bit of a bug, love?

Yeah, it's called smoking. Sorry.

'Sall right.

Everybody's quiet. Alvy's fingertip is purple. Feels like Mrs. Chatwin's about to say Well then, nice to have met you, but Dad – C'mon, thinks Jacob – says Old town treatin you well, then?

Well, says Mrs. Chatwin, big change from what we were used to in Alberta – Dad blinks – but we're doing okay, eh, Alv?

Alvy shrugs while he undoes the tie.

His girlfriend keeps him pretty busy these days, says his mum, but Jacob there, he was, he was a great friend for Alvy to make. New town and all. It was good they had so much in common.

I didnae realize.

Mrs. Chatwin nods. I'm sure, she says, you're very proud of Jacob. What with the running and all.

The kid does all right.

And you, John, you're an ambulance driver I hear.

'Deed I am. Yourself?

Me? Not working, not right now. I, my hus, well, what you do, that's wonderful. Helping people.

Dad shrugs. Keeps, he says, the wolf from the door. Then he nods at Mrs. Chatwin's cart and says Got the whole garden in there.

Oh, I love to cook. Eh, Alvy?

Alvy opens his mouth, but Mrs. Chatwin's eyes flare like matches. Say, two of you oughta come over for dinner!

Alvy and Jacob's eyes lock.

And Dad talks like a mouthful of mushrooms. Eh, uh, mwa, don't want to bother you, like.

Nonsense. We'd love to have you over, eh, Alv?

Yeah, sure. But Alvy steps behind his mum, gives Jacob a look over her shoulder.

So, while Dad shifts his weight from foot to foot, Jacob says That'd be great, Mrs. Chatwin, thanks for the invite.

Mrs. Chatwin's eyebrows say *Well?*

And Dad says Suppose it's settled then.

Super, says Mrs. Chatwin. Saturday all right?

Suits me fine.

Alvy says Can Gail come?

Oh, Alvy, says Mrs. Chatwin, you can go one night, for Pete's sake. Spend some time with your friend.

Alvy nods like he's dead and you're lifting his chin with your finger.

Well then, we'll see you boys Saturday. Say, six?

Six it is, Dad says.

Alvy follows his mum off and she gravelly-laughs about her cart's bum wheel.

Dad looks at Jacob sideways and out the corner of his mouth says Emphysema's gonnae get her.

Maybe she'll quit. You and Mum did.

Wanna walk home?

No.

Then shut it.

Half the night Jacob lies there. Feels like he could be sick.

At school the next day, he writes a note in art. Hands it to Cracks and whispers Chatwin, pass it on, but Mrs. Bunko traps it halfway. All it says is *Recess, talk?* but Bunko crumples it when Melissa Fowler finks. Jacob has to stand in the corner.

Morning and afternoon recess he tries to find Alvy, but he's good at finding hiding places with Gail to neck. Friday he sees them between classes down the hall, and you can tell – the way they both look at him – Alvy's talking to her about tomorrow. But the way Gail puts her hand on his chest, how she looks at Jacob and back at Alvy – it's like she's saying You should, Alvy, he was your best friend. And Alvy nods.

For now, that's good enough. But somehow Spielman finds out what's going on – everybody tells everybody except Jacob everything in this stupid school – and every time Jacob looks over at him in class he's wearing an idiot grin and sliding his finger in and out his fist.

At afternoon recess Jacob stays in the washroom for a while, hands either side of the sink. Spits in it. Has a look at himself. And says You're for it, Dean, and fuck your flowers, too. Spits again. But thinks it's not worth a trip to Shits Himself, so he waits till after school. Runs ahead, and hides behind a tree on Oliver. And here they come, Dean and Cracks, arguing about Guy Lafleur and Mike Bossy and who's better. Jacob never learned to skate and who gives a frig about hockey. He crouches, decides to go for the legs. And, at the last second, he ... can't move. They don't even see him till he's running in the other direction. Cracks yells his name, but Jacob just keeps going.

And keeps going past the six-mile mark Saturday morning. Dad doesn't break stride. Full of piss and vinegar, are you?

Just an extra half mile out, Dad.

So, this is your first thirteener, then?

Guess so.

A half marathon.

Jacob nods.

There's one comin up down in Peterborough this January. Snofest. Are you for it?

Sure, says Jacob, and he picks it up.

Dad, too.

By the turn they're both quiet. Focused. This isn't a run. This is a race. Shoulder to shoulder they stay. Gimme an inch, says Dad, and I'll take a mile.

So Jacob edges by.

Smartarse, eh? Dad draws even, moves in front.

Jacob tucks in. Let Dad fight the wind.

No talking at all now. Just breathing. Fluids. Head up. Mile Ten split, 6:40, and Jacob can feel it. Can hear it in Dad's breath. He has him. Too many nights out. Too many mornings off. But Jacob lets on like it's a slog, stays right where he is, tucked in, till they pass the Murph's mailbox and turn off the Sterling Road. Then, the bits coming – Mrs. Chatwin's face, Mum's face, Best Couple – he takes off and pounds pounds pounds down Bridge Street hill. Dad on his heels. But fading.

When he gets his breath back, Dad says his Achilles tendon was hurting, may be time for new shoes. Jacob says Thought something was wrong, but thinks that come Snofest, he'll beat Dad by a mile.

On the way they stop at the liquor store first –
It's a courtesy, son, always remember that – where Dad buys two
bottles of Piat d'Or, one white, one red, and a couple of poppies
from the Legion man out front. Get this on you. Now, where is
their place again?

Near our old one. On Booth.

Let's get a move on then. We'll be late.

Dad whistles on the way. Nods at Jacob to join in. He fakes it.
Dad doesn't notice.

Dad. *Dad.*

This it?

Jacob nods.

Wait a minute, I've been here.

When?

Ages ago. On a call. It was what's-her-name used to live here.

Jacob shrugs.

Poor wee thing, what was her name? Agnes or something.
Had to take the pen right out her fingers.

She was writing?

She was dead. Right there in the armchair. Poor wee thing.
She'd been writin a letter to her husband, dead as well.

At the same time?

No. Long ago. She forgot was all. Senile, like. Dad makes
circles by his temple. Anyway, he says, shifting the bag to his other
arm, shall we?

Dad …

C'mon.

I wanna go home.

You'd better be fucken jokin me.

I'm not, I'm not feelin well.

Boy, *get* up that walk.

At the door, Dad says And get that look off your face. This woman's cooked us dinner, 'sakes, and you will fuckingwell *eat* it, hear me?

Jacob nods, and Dad, shaking his head, knocks. See, he says, when I get you home ...

But here comes Alvy, blurry through the glass. Dad elbows Jacob just before the door opens. Hi.

Hi.

Come in.

Thank you, lad.

They doff their coats – Shoes as well, boy – and Alvy puts them in the closet. Follow me, he says.

The house, Jacob thinks, stinks like a cheese factory. Or glue. Dad notices it, too, but on the way down the hall he says Smells lovely.

Alvy leads them into the kitchen. Mrs. Chatwin's just closed the oven door. She smooths the front of her apron, and says Evening, gents.

Evening, Alice.

Don't you look dapper, John.

Eh, thanks. For the table.

Piat d'Or. Lovely. I'll get the white in the fridge. Set yourself down, boys, dinner won't be long.

It's blue-cheese lasagna, says Alvy.

Oh, says Dad, like he's had it a hundred times.

There's blue, says Jacob, *cheese?*

Dad throws Jacob a quick *shut it* look, and Alvy says Mould. His mum opens a window – it's a hundred reeking degrees in here – and puts the red Piat d'Or on the table. It's set with real plates plus two tall candles in holders shaped like angels.

Beer to start, John?

Dad says That would be lovely, and Alvy says It's delicious.

What is, says Jacob.

Coke for you boys?

Yes, please. Blue cheese is delicious.

Could I please have milk instead? How can it be blue?

From the mould.

Sure you don't want Coke? We got lots.

Jacob looks at Dad. His eyebrows shrug. No, says Jacob, milk's good.

Wear a moustache, says Mrs. Chatwin. She gets two Exports and frosty mugs, pours Alvy a big glass of Coke with ice and puts a new bag of milk in the pitcher. Clips the corner and pours a glass while Alvy, Dad and Jacob just sit there and look at the tablecloth.

Jacob, Alvy, there you go, and John, there we are, cheers.

Cheers to you, love, and thanks for having us.

C'mon, boys, says Mrs. Chatwin.

Ka-clink-clunk-clink but Alvy won't look up, and just takes a little sip. Dad, too. Mrs. Chatwin takes a pretty good haul. Shouldn't be long, she says, looking at the stove. Would you like to start with salad, tide us over?

With the meal is fine with me, says Dad. He takes a bigger sip.

Okay then. Well. I'm sure glad you boys could make it.

Our pleasure, says Dad.

Mom? says Alvy.

Yeah, hon?

Can I go feed the guys?

Alvy. We've got company.

Just a few minutes.

Well, I guess so, says Mrs. Chatwin. She looks at Dad and says Alvy's just got a new, well, it's better if he tells you about it. Jacob, why don't you go on up with him?

Alvy freezes halfway out of his chair.

And Jacob looks at Dad. Gets the okay. Checks his shoulder when he's almost out the kitchen because Mrs. Chatwin says Mind if I smoke?

Nae bother to me.

Trying to quit, but it's hard.

Aye.

C'mon, poky, says Alvy.

On their way up the stairs, Jacob's heart thumps. Alvy's bedroom. Maybe he feels up Gail McBride in there, or fingers her Mound of Venus.

You can come in.

It's pitch-black.

Just wait.

Alvy *tak* hits a switch. Blue light, from a little lamp beside his bed. Alvy says Groovy, eh?

Jacob's eyes adjust, and he sees drawings on the walls – dissected animals and superheroes – and What the frig is that?

Birdcage, says Alvy, *shh*.

Not that, *that*. Jacob points to the fish tank beside the covered cage.

That's Mobius, says Alvy.

Freaky, says Jacob, and he bends, has a look. About the size of a goldfish, but it's red, with big fins that billow like cloaks.

Bait a splend ins, says Alvy.

Say again?

Betta splendens. Siamese fighting fish.

Fighting fish?

Never seen one before?

Jacob shakes his head. Stares at the fish. What do they fight?

Other fish.

Why?

Territorial. Can only put one in a tank this small. Two'd tear each other apart. Even a female. Unless she's ready to spawn. If she isn't, the male'd bite her to death.

How do you know he's male?

Asked.

Where?

Pet store.

Where?

Peterborough.

When'd you go?

Last week. Saw *Amityville Horror* with Gail.

Oh. Jacob looks back at the fishbowl, goes to *tink* the glass but Alvy says *Don't*.

Sorry.

'Sokay. Better if you do this. Alvy goes to his bedside table, comes back with a lady's makeup mirror. Turns on the normal light. That'll wake the boys, he says, but no problem. Check this out. Alvy cracks open the mirror like a clam, blows makeup off, holds it to the bowl.

Holy jumpin.

Thinks it's another fish, says Alvy. He closes the mirror *clackt* and Jacob starts to say Do it again, but the birdcage peeps, and through the cover Alvy says Hell-o there, widdle guys, then he looks back at Jacob. Wanna see 'em?

Sure.

Alvy slips the cover off the cage, tosses it on his bed.

The birds look stuffed. But then the one on the right ruffles and chirps.

Alvy opens the cage, reaches in – *flutter flutter chirp chirp* – and then the bird is in his fist. He holds the little head to his lips. Smooches it and says How's the widdle guy?

Peep.

Wanna hold him?

Don't know how.

Like this. It's easy.

Might peck me or something.

No he won't. Alvy takes Jacob's wrist and puts the bird in his hand. Just hold him, Jacob, don't wring him out.

Sorry, says Jacob, his heart going almost as fast as the little one beating against his thumb.

'Sokay, says Alvy, he won't hurt you.

Jacob doesn't know if Alvy means him or the bird. Here, Alvy, take him back.

'Kay, just, yeah, *there* we go. He smooches the little head again, and back in the cage it goes *flap-flap-flap* on the perch. *Chirp.*

Guess we should head back down, says Alvy.

Yeah, guess so.

You cold or something?

No.

Alvy slides the cover back on, turns off the light and the blue lamp, says Goodnight, boys.

They don't talk on the way down the stairs, just look at each other sideways when they hear the laughing from the kitchen. When they come in, Mrs. Chatwin's wiping the corner of her eye with her knuckle. Jacob, she says, your dad's been telling me army stories.

Alvy says What army were you in?

Black Watch, son. Scottish regiment.

Ever have to shoot anyone?

Mrs. Chatwin's mouth drops. Alvy *Chatwin*, she says.

'Sall right, says Dad. Not me, son, he says. Just dug ditches, was all. Then he winks at Mrs. Chatwin and they laugh a little more. Suck back beer. Their second one each. Well, says Alvy's mum, that oughta do it on the lasagna. Hungry?

Starving, says Alvy.

Me, too, says Jacob after Dad gives him a look and says You bet, Alice, smells delicious.

Mrs. Chatwin leaves the oven door open, like a sauna in here, when she dishes out the gunk.

There you be, Jacob. If it's too rich you let me know.

Looks lovely, says Dad. Now, shall I pour the –

Dad puts the Piat d'Or down when Mrs. Chatwin bows her head and says Alvy?

Mom ...

Alvy Chatwin. She cracks an eye and says Believe it or not, John, Alvy does like to say grace.

Course, says Dad, and he winks at Jacob when Mrs. Chatwin and Alvy have their eyes closed.

Go ahead, dear.

Dear God, thank you for this great food, and for Jacob and Mr. McKnight. We hope that everyone can partake of thy bounty, even Russians, amen.

Dad's got his hands clasped tight and his eyes shut like devotion but he almost laughs, and Mrs. Chatwin says Well, that wasn't your usual, dear, but it was lovely, thank you.

Let's eat, says Alvy, and he cuts the lasagna with his fork, shovels it in.

Dad pours wine for himself and Mrs. Chatwin. To your health, love.

And you, John.

Ting.

Your dad was telling me about Cyprus, Jacob, I'd never even heard of it.

Dad starts in on the Isle o' Love business, and Jacob tries a forkful. Doesn't want to swallow it. Gulps milk. As Dad goes on about Greeks and Turks and you wouldn't believe the things you see and Mrs. Chatwin chews and nods, Jacob decides to take one more bite, a big one, then leave the rest and eat his salad. Alvy's gobbling away like the stuff is Kraft Dinner. Asks for seconds and without looking at him Mrs. Chatwin says Help yourself. You were saying, John?

Jacob forces the second bite down. It's like vinegar and glue. He chugs milk. So *hot* in here. Eyes the salad. Spinach. Bits of egg in it. Jacob pushes them to the side. Lets a quiet burp out the corner of his mouth and eats a few leaves. Alvy wolfs his. Hon, says Mrs. Chatwin when Dad stops talking and takes a bite, no one's gonna take that away from you, you know.

Boy loves his mum's cooking, says Dad.

Then everybody looks at Jacob's plate.

Everything all right? says Mrs. Chatwin.

Fine.

We're not used to the gourmet fare, says Dad like he's talking to bill collectors. Might be a bit rich for the boy.

No, says Jacob, it's okay, really. And he scoops a big forkful of lasagna. Gets it down, but wishes it was summertime, not November, then it'd be just Dad and him out on the patio with corn on the cob or barbecue chicken down at Neily's. Tossing the football. Flowers everywhere. Not fake poppies and mouldy cheese. And won't Dad just shut up. Stop drinking and shut up, Dad. He talks and he talks and he talks. Mrs. Chatwin says something about a mine in Alberta that was buried under half a mountain but

Dad jumps in and goes on about Mount Cruachan and working mine rescue and Mrs. Chatwin says You were a miner, *too*? O aye. And both their faces look like slapped asses, More wine, John? Ach, why the hell no.

Mrs. Chatwin upends the bottle over Dad's glass. Holds it – drip, drip – and says 'Nother one where that came from.

Jacob swallows burp and burn. Pats his belly like he's had a good feed.

Mrs. Chatwin pops the cork and asks him if he wants some more.

Think I'm full, Mrs. Chatwin.

We've got pie, she says, then covers her mouth and hiccups. Mercy me pardon, aren't I the lady.

Look like one from here, Dad says.

And Jacob – *gwlah* – slaps both hands over his mouth.

Mom! Alvy says, but Mrs. Chatwin's already got Jacob by the shoulders. C'mon dear let's go come on come with me you'll be all right. And he's through the living room half-bent and heaving and slipping up the stairs then – Here honey, here – finally the bathroom and Mrs. Chatwin gets the lid up just in time. Rubs his back. Jacob spits, feels Dad behind him, and his back bends like a bow.

Gross me out, says Alvy.

You, says Mrs. Chatwin. Downstairs.

But –

Down-*stairs*.

Alvy clomps off.

And Jacob blinks, breathes, spits.

Mrs. Chatwin flushes it down.

Dad says You sure that's it, boy?

Jacob nods.

I'm awfully sorry, Alice.

Don't you worry one bit, John, these things happen.

Best we be on our way, get this one home and intae his bed.

You sure that's the best? Jacob, you ready to walk, hon?

Jacob nods, tries to stand.

Easy, honey.

Dad's face, disgusted.

It's all *right*, John. Now listen, why don't we lay him down, in Alvy's room, I'll get you a nice cool cloth, Jacob, let him rest a bit.

'Sall right, says Dad, I'll see to him.

Mrs. Chatwin stays in Dad's way. John, he'll be better able to go home once he's laid down. Now let's have a cup of coffee and give him some time to breathe. Jacob, honey, I know that meal was pretty rich. Sorry, hon.

Was my fault, Mrs. Chatwin, I'm sorry.

Don't be. You follow me now, lie down a bit, you'll be right as rain.

Mrs. Chatwin takes Jacob's arm above the elbow and walks him past Dad to Alvy's room. Doesn't turn the light on. Sits him on the edge of the bed and says Go on, sweetie, lie down now.

Jacob lies back, hands on his belly.

Be right back, says Mrs. Chatwin.

Jacob hears the washroom sink running, and Dad's footfalls. His head, half shadow, around the door frame and his voice like a night hiss. Twenty minutes, boy, do you *hear* me, twenty minutes and on those fucking *feet*.

Back in the hallway Dad says Thanks for seeing to the boy. And then he whispers something.

Mrs. Chatwin comes in, washcloth in one hand, wastebin in the other. Sets the bin by the bed, says It's there if you need it, then lays the cloth, cool, across Jacob's forehead.

How's that?

Good.

Not too cold?

No.

You just relax now, hon. *Peck* on the cheek. Door closed?

Open, please.

Call if you need me.

'Kay. Jacob waits till she's on the stairs, rolls over, holds the cloth over his whole face.

Sits up. Blinks. Doesn't remember where he is until the bird chirps.

Jacob?

Holy *shit*, Alvy, you scared me.

Your dad's going.

I'm dead, Alv.

But Alvy says nothing, and Jacob still can't see his face clear. Just hears the creaky footsteps going back down the hall.

On the way home Dad says nothing except *Keep* up. It's like Jacob's not even there. Inside, he gets ready for it, but Dad just stares at him. His face, divided – half mad, half sad.

Dad, I'm –

Don't talk to me.

I'm –

G'wan to your bed. *G'wan* I said.

Jacob leaves his clothes in a pile. No PJs. Just sits in the middle of the bed, holding the pillow against his belly. Hears Dad making a drink, pacing the kitchen. Then he puts down his drink, and picks up the phone.

Eh, hallo, it's John ... Hope you don't mind my callin ... Just wanted tae apologize again, like ... He'll be all right.

Then Dad starts whispering, and Jacob drops the pillow. Takes the poppy off his jacket. Pokes his thumb until it bleeds. Hides under the covers when Dad hangs up, thumb in his mouth. Stays that way for a while after Dad's bedroom door bangs shut. Then throws the covers off, a T-shirt over his lamp, and gets *The Anatomy Coloring Book*. He flips pages, looks at all the bits, almost a whole year now, that he coloured. The spine, the muscles and bones of the lower leg, the elbow. The bones of the skull, the Child of Uncertain Years. He stares at the dying saint eyes, the sagging mouth. Wants it to move, to speak something, to tell him what to do. But it's just a picture, quiet as cemeteries.

Jacob swings his legs over the edge. It's light already. He blinks. Knuckles his eyes. Waits.

His tummy feels all right.

Gear on, he waits in the kitchen. Dad doesn't come out until almost ten. Doesn't look tired. He looks old. What's with the gear, he says.

I feel okay, Dad.

That so?

Jacob nods.

Ten minutes, says Dad.

You're not going?

Where?

To the cenotaph. Today's the eleventh.

Yeah, well. Always next year, isn't there?

Guess so.

Ten minutes.

It's more like twenty, but Dad looks better when he comes out the washroom. Doesn't look so good two miles out. Thick spit at the corners of his mouth. Slow it down, fucksakes.

Sorry. Where you going?

Five'll do it.

Supposed to be six.

Well it's five and let's get it fuckingwell done. I want to talk to you.

Jacob makes the turn. Catches up. Settles in, looking sideways at Dad, back at the road, back at Dad. How you feeling?

Me? You're the one saw his dinner twice.

Jacob eyes the edge of town. Wants it fuckingwell done as well, this run, this month, this winter.

Hey, you hear me?

Pardon?

You, last night. Great show of thanks, that was.

Couldn't help it, Dad.

Don't imagine we'll be gettin another invite any time soon.

Jacob picks up the pace and says Fine with me.

What was that?

Dad draws alongside and – *wham* – elbows Jacob in the ribs. Fine with you, is it? *Wham*.

Jacob stumbles, catches himself.

What if it's no fine with me? Eh? *Wham*.

Stop it.

Made of sugar?

Stop it.

You're telling me now, is that it?

Jacob lengthens his stride.

I'll tell *you* when to fuckingwell stop.

Through the breath, coming now in fits and starts, through his knocking teeth, Jacob says What's wrong, miss her?

Mind your fucken *mouth*, boy.

Jacob turns and takes big strides backwards. *Do* you? Do you want Mrs. Chatwin as a girlfriend?

I'll want what I fuckingwell want.

Do you even *know* it's Mum's birthday in a week?

Dad's mouth folds and snarls like a bashed car's face. Then he charges. You, here!

Jacob turns, bears down.

Fine, *fuck* off then.

Jacob turns and scissor-steps. I *will*. I *will* fuck off!

What's keeping you?

I will! I'll run and –

What, says Dad, stopping, breathing hard. You'll what?

Jacob stops and makes fists and hammers the air. I'll *run*, he says.

Go *on* then.

Jacob jerks his thumb. I'll *hitch*-hike –

Do what you like.

– all the *way*, all the way to Alberta.

Dad's face almost dies.

213

I *will* at least she has her own teeth and I won't have to run down this stupid fucksakes road I hate it –

Enough.

– I hate running and I hate –

Dad's eyes bulge. He charges.

– you! Bastard asshole, says Jacob, and then he runs hard.

Boy!

Jacob pumps his arms, lifts his legs, breathes.

Jacob! No!

A blur in the corner of Jacob's eye.

Son! No!

And the *tikkita-tikkita* of claws against road.

Jacob checks his shoulder.

And sees the dog. Coming for him.

Dad!

Stop, son, face him!

Imagining teeth, the torn-out tendon and the dog on him, Jacob turns. Here comes Dad, but the dog's well ahead. It stops two strides shy of Jacob, slobber and gnash.

Dad! Help me!

Dad stops well behind the dog. Holds out his hand. Son, listen to me. You're all right, he'd have gone for you.

Help me!

I don't want to spook him into –

Jacob backs up.

No, son! says Dad when the dog snarls and lunges, stops, takes one step, two. Son, stand up straight and scream at the bastard. Show him who's boss.

Dad!

Do it, boy.

The dog barks and growls and gnashes like it's attacking the air.

Dad!

Do it! But stand where y'are, don't charge him, just wave your arms and –

Leave me ALON–

The word disappears in scream and Dad and the dog and the road dissolve and everything's blank for a blink till Dad – I'll fucken *kell* ya – takes two huge strides and hoofs the dog's haunch like a soccer ball. GET the fuck gone with you, bastard!

Again Dad goes to put the boot in but the dog's limping off and yelping like it's caught under a car and can't die.

And Dad bends double, hands on knees. *Phooh, phooh.* He spits and stands and says I've a *fucken* mind to do the same thing to Murphy's head as well. That fucking *asshole*. Let something like that run free, Jesus suffer *fuck*. You hear me, asshole? Dad walks back to the laneway. The dog looks back but keeps running off. Yeah, I'll cave your fucking *mouth* in next time. You hear me, Murphy? I'll be paying you a visit, bampot!

Dad?

But he pays no attention, starts walking up the drive – Dad, no – with his hands like a megaphone. You hear me, asshole? I'm for ya!

Dad waits.

Except for Jacob's breath, it's dead quiet.

Dad looks, looks, says *Ach* like he's coughing up hair and walks back to the road. Slaps the mailbox. Fucken coward, he says. Let's go, boy.

Jacob points.

Dad whips round.

The Murph's car. Coming.

Son. On with you.

Dad.

Go!

Jacob jumps, jogs a few steps, looks back – the car's stopping – jogs more, stops. Looks. There's another dog in the back seat. And it's going bonkers.

Dad spreads his arms. Well come on, fucker! Or are you going to sic your mutt on me, eh? I'll put a boot in its face, too. Come on!

Dad!

But he doesn't listen. And the Murph gets out. Closes the door in the dog's face. Just stands there, his back to Dad, looking at the barking dog. Then turns round. Now look, he says, but Dad says You're done, asshole. And moves in. *Jab, jab, jab*, and the Murph's head bounces back, back, back. He gets his hands up, takes a swing, but he doesn't want it. Dad ducks and slides back. Come on, ya fucker, *jab*. I said come *on*. Two more on the mouth, then he digs in the ribs and – the furious dog's claws raking the windscreen – puts one in the temple, another on the jaw. The Murph flops like Heart Attack Annie over the hood of the car. Looks over at Jacob. His busted face. Dad leans right into it. You're a waste of my *time*, asshole. Then he *slaps* the windshield *Shut* yer mug or I'll be back with a rifle! Grabs the Murph by his jacket, holds him there on the edge of the hood. Doesn't even punch him anymore. Just open-hands him. *You*, and your *dogs*, stay a-*way*, from the boy or I *swear* I'll fucken –

Dad!

The Murph bear-hugs him. Roars and shakes and lifts him. And takes him down.

Jacob runs closer. Get off him!

Dad gets a knee in but the Murph's too heavy. Rolls Dad. Gets an arm round his neck.

And Jacob runs. Right at them. Aims for the kidney. And stomps.

The Murph screams and reaches.

And Dad gets hold of an ear. Turns it like a screw – How's that, fucker? – and the Murph rolls off. Dad drags him up and slams him over the hood of the car and gets a fistful of hair and slams him again and the dog Jacob swears it's coming right through that windshield.

Dad!

Slam.

Dad, no!

Slam.

Leave him alone!

Dad stops. Looks at Jacob. *This*? he says, leave *this* the fuck alone? Get out of here, boy, I'm telling you.

I didn't fucken do anything, says the Murph, and he's almost crying.

Shut your mouth.

I swear, I never touched him.

What in fuck are you telling me?

Dad ...

Shut up, boy!

I never touched –

I don't give a fuck about all that. Just you and your mutts keep away from *my* boy, y'hear me? Eh? Y'hear me? Dad gives him one more shake, not hard, and says I mean it, I'll be back here with a fucken rifle if I ever see them again.

The Murph nods, looks at Jacob like he didn't deserve this but still is sorry, sorry, sorry.

Now go *on*, says Dad, go and get yourself cleaned up. And don't think you're getting in that fucken car. Walk and let that mutt calm down.

The Murph rolls off the hood. Shoves his hair over his ears. Starts walking.

Dad watches him for a bit. Wipes his face. Turns round and sees the dark patches down Jacob's sweats.

Fists shoved down the front to keep the stinking prickly wet off him, Jacob, shivering, says he couldn't help it, it just happened and he couldn't help it.

Here now – Dad walks forward, Jacob steps back – here now, 'sall right. His hand round the back of Jacob's neck, Dad says Look at me, and rubs. 'Sall right now, he says, all over.

Jacob leans in, shivering, everywhere shivering, Dad's shoulder hard against his cheekbone.

Come on, lad, c'mon now. It's all over, I said. You did well.

I got so scared.

Me as well.

You?

Yeah me. Fucken petrified.

Jacob's mouth spreads wide wide open, and he shoves his lips hard against Dad's neck to stop the sound from coming out.

C'mon now, says Dad, his hand still hugging Jacob's neck, time we got home. Can you make it?

Jacob shakes his head.

'Sall right. We'll walk for now. Someone comes along, we'll hitch a wee ride. C'mon now.

Strings of snot and slobber stretch then break when Jacob lifts his head and says he's sorry.

Sorry what for?

Everything.

Ach, we're all right.

They walk. Check their shoulders. But nothing's there. Old road's quiet today, says Dad.

Jacob nods. Pulls the pee cling free of his legs. He wants a bath. Steaming Cream of Wheat, with honey in it. Scrambled eggs with soldiers, and two cups of tea. Dad?

Yes, Jacob?

I can do it.

Eh?

Home. I can run.

Hang on a minute, son, I think we're in luck.

Jacob looks back. A green van. Dad hangs his thumb out.

No, Dad.

You sure?

Jacob nods.

On its way by, the van honks and Dad waves.

Who was it? says Jacob.

No idea. Knew us, though.

Everybody knows us.

Oh aye, famous we are.

C'mon, Dad. Jacob starts jogging.

And Dad says You go on ahead, kid, I'm pooped.

ACKNOWLEDGEMENTS

Thanks to Sarah Heller for agreeing to represent me and my work. This novel, *Down Sterling Road*, wouldn't know its current form without the effort, faith and care of two remarkable women: Alana Wilcox, my editor, and Aritha van Herk, my teacher.

These acknowledgements would be travestied without thanking another remarkable woman, the most remarkable one I know, Violette Hiebert, for her art, and for her heart, her heart.

Thanks as well to Greg Gerrard and the staff of Pages on Kensington in Calgary, a fine group of booksellers who freed me from significant portions of the scholarship monies awarded me by the University of Calgary's Faculty of Graduate Studies, and its Department of English. I thank both of those bodies profoundly, and hope I have added what honour I can to an already distinguished writing program.

Down Sterling Road took its first strides in English 598 (2000–2001), an eight-month fiction-writing workshop at the University of Calgary. Participants included Marika Deliyannides, W. Mark Giles, Jacky Honnet, Sam Pane, Anne Sorbie and Gisèle Villeneuve. All of these folks are fine writers, and all of them deserve my gratitude – for their guidance, for their friendship.

Calgary has been a real home these past five years, not only because of its tenacious, vibrant writing community, but also because I was reunited here with members of my family too little seen and too rarely thanked: my mum, Olive Gerstman, and my sister, Janet Morgan.

Lists can efface as much as they include, but everyone in this list counts, and I thank them sincerely: Paul Anderson, William Ashline, Frances Batycki, Stan Bevington, Neil Burgess and family, Timothy Findley, Jay Gamble, Barry Grenon, Richard Harrison, Stephen Henighan, the Hiebert family, Ken Jacobsen, Jon Kertzer, Robert Kroetsch, Stephanie Mason, Christina Palassio, Roberta Rees, Stephen and Diane Rohleder, Stuart Ross, Ryan Simpson, Stephen Ross Smith, Wayne K. Spear, Nancy Tousley, Mario Trono, Harry Vandervlist, and Martin Watson.

Adrian Michael Kelly was born in Timmins, Ontario, but grew up in Campbellford. After taking a BA in English at Trent, and an MA in English from Queen's, he lived in South Korea, Switzerland and Italy. He then moved to Calgary to complete his doctorate. His short fiction and literary journalism have appeared in *The Queen's Quarterly*, *filling Station*, *paperbytes*, *Ffwd*, *Alberta Views* and the *Calgary Herald*.

Typeset in Scala and printed and bound at the Coach House on
bpNichol Lane, 2005

Edited and designed by Alana Wilcox
Cover photo and author photo by Violette Hiebert
Cover design by Stan Bevington

Coach House Books
401 Huron St. on bpNichol Lane
Toronto, Ontario
M5S 2G5

416 979 2217
800 367 6360

mail@chbooks.com
www.chbooks.com